Polyamorous Love Song

Polyamorous Love Song

Jacob Wren

BOOKTHUG · TORONTO
2014

FIRST EDITION

Copyright © Jacob Wren, 2014

Cover image by Matthew Palladino. Used with permission.

The production of this book was made possible through the generous assistance of the Canada Council for the Arts and the Ontario Arts Council.

LIBRARY AND ARCHIVES CANADA CATALOGUING IN PUBLICATION

Wren, Jacob, author
    Polyamorous love song / Jacob Wren.

(Department of narrative studies ; no. 12)
Issued in print and electronic formats.
ISBN 978-1-77166-030-3 (pbk.).--ISBN 978-1-77166-037-2 (html)

    I. Title. II. Series: Department of narrative studies ; no. 12

PS8595.R454P64 2014   C813'.54   C2013-908721-4
                                           C2013-908722-2

PRINTED IN CANADA

Contents

1. Artists Are Self-Absorbed

And my theory about professional artists was as follows: Artists are not necessarily the most creative or inspired individuals in any given community. Instead they are those individuals most willing to exploit their own creativity and inspiration, most willing to gain personal profit from their unconscious and its emanations, those with the most missionary zeal for the dissemination of their own idiosyncratic perspectives. Questions of pure creativity clearly lay elsewhere.

Like most of us I once knew someone who was one of the most creative, strange, deeply interesting people I would ever meet. I'm not sure he actually liked me very much but I admired him and therefore he humoured me. Before beginning this book I emailed him to ask if it would be all right for me to write about him and also to write about some of the things he has said to me over the years. He said no, that it was not all right. I then asked if it would be all right to write about him if I were to avoid any mention of his real name. Once again he said no, he would not be comfortable with such a situation. I then asked if it would be all right to write about him if I were to avoid using his real name and also alter key details of his story so as to render it virtually unrecognizable. Once again he said no, and also mentioned that he hoped I would not come to him with any further requests. He was easily one of the most creative people I have ever met, his thoughts and work far more compelling than that of most of the other, allegedly more professional, artists I have encountered over the years. I am tempted to explain more about him in what follows, which would of course be absolutely contrary to his clearly stated wishes. However, then I would not only be exploiting my own creativity, I would also be exploiting his. And he has clearly told me not to. Sadly, the theory I proposed in the first paragraph will have to remain unillustrated.

Sometimes when I run out of ideas I attempt to write down my dreams. In one dream, which has visited me sporadically over the course of many years, often arriving on nights when I least expect it, or on nights when I have completely forgotten I have ever had such a dream in the first place, there is a secret society the existence of which only circulates in the vaguest of rumours. Of course immediately I want to join. This desire to join is so strong within me it rapidly becomes something of a piercing obsession. It remains unclear to me if the organization I so desperately want to join is an organized group that runs things from behind the scenes or only a group that makes the lives of those people who actually run things somehow more difficult. I make many enquiries and eventually come to understand what I have to do. There is a door and you knock on the door and someone eventually opens it. You explain to the man that opens the door that you have new ideas that will contribute greatly to the secrecy and efficacy of the organization and he asks you what exactly these 'new' ideas are. And this next part is incredibly important: You must absolutely refuse to tell him. No matter how much he asks or how much he pleads you continue to say nothing. In this way you create a sense of mystery and a desire, on his part, to know more. It seems like a stupid strategy but within the strange logic of the dream you are surprised how well it actually works. Then there is a period of several years when you are somehow aware that you are loosely associated with this secret society even though you have yet to witness any concrete evidence of its existence. Still, you have made the first step, a certain degree of progress, and you continue to have hope.

I am very nervous to write down my dreams, somehow plagued by a nagging feeling that one's unconscious should not be exploited for artistic ends. This was one of the topics I often used to speak about with Paul (not his real name, and I'm sorry Paul, I know you didn't want me to write about you and I am writing about you anyway – but I suppose this will be neither my first nor my last betrayal). Because art itself is a kind of dream and to portray a dream within a work of art or to transform one's actual dreams into works of art seems redundant. But not only redundant. For in many ways one's dreams represent aspects of one's deepest self, and there is no reason to publicize such things carelessly.

There is a kind of dream therapy in which one takes turns placing oneself inside each of the different characters within a remembered dream, since each of these characters simply represents different aspects of the self. So if you were to have a dream in which you were beaten by a police officer, you would put yourself in the place of the police officer and intuit what he thinks and does as if such thoughts and actions were only other aspects of your self, and as if within your unconscious you are never only the one being beaten but also the one doing the beating. Just like in life one is never wholly innocent, one must continually feel implicated, always take on aspects of the collective guilt.

So several years passed and, though I felt confident I had remained implicated within, if not the inner circle, at least the periphery of the global secret society, I still had no further concrete or factual information as to the intricacies of its machinations. Occasionally I would hear something, a snippet of conversation from the next table in a restaurant, or read something, a note left in my mailbox at work or a single sentence in a larger unrelated article that subtly hinted at some ongoing, hidden network. But you realize that you have been told to wait and therefore all you can do is wait, confident, or at least cautiously hopeful, that sooner or later they will call upon you and you will be given the opportunity to slip upwards in the ranks towards an eventual goal of penetrating the inner circle.

In the dream you are married and having an affair. And your wife is also having an affair and you begin to suspect that the man your wife is having an affair with is in fact quite deeply implicated in the secret society that you remain a casual, loosely affiliated member of. At night, in bed, you think of confronting her about this – not about the affair, but rather whether she can use her sexual connection with this man to help you, her husband, advance within the ranks. You most certainly don't want her to stop having the affair, not only because you would have to stop your own affair, which you seem to be enjoying immensely, but also because then your only real lead, your one opportunity for further advancement within the secret sect, would rapidly evaporate. You are afraid that if you raise the question with your wife she will misunderstand you, think that you are only confronting her in order to force her to break off the affair. And somehow you have to do all of this without letting on that you are aware of the existence of the secret society, since you are not sure whether she knows about it, and if you were to reveal it to someone who is not supposed to know, it would once again harm your chances for further advancement.

Fortunately, one night while you are still paralyzed by indecision, unsure how to breach the topic, your wife assists: First she tells you that she knows you are having an affair but that it is perfectly all right since she is also having an affair and, if you agree, she proposes that you both continue. You instantly agree. Then she tells you that, although she doesn't understand why, the man she is having an affair with would like to invite you to a meeting. She gives you the time and address and for a few hours you couldn't possibly be happier.

Paul had a motorcycle. (Actually he didn't, but it is my hope that this detail will render those who know him unable to identify who I am referring to since, as I have already mentioned, that is his explicit wish. More specifically, since I have already defied his most explicit wish, I am hoping this is the next best thing: a compromise he will still disagree with but have to settle for.) I would see him on his motorcycle, driving around at night, consequently lost in his own spiralling thoughts, as if trying to figure out a complex problem that was meant only for him and him alone, or perhaps thinking nothing, his inner world merely the distant, idealized projection of what I might be thinking if I were him. Sometimes, on these nights, I would flag him down and we would talk for a while. Or go for a drink. Or he would

11

park his motorcycle and we would walk. He would tell me things and I would listen, and everything he said would strike me as brilliant and alluring. And yet at other times I would let him ride by, certain that he had not noticed me, not wanting to interfere with what I assumed were his endlessly fascinating inner monologues, since in the end, even when we were to drink or talk, I couldn't help but feel his thoughts were meant only for himself, were being shared with me reluctantly, almost against his will.

One time he asked me this: If you were to take all of your thoughts, all of the thoughts that you'd ever had, and divide them into two piles, with one pile being all the thoughts that you've had that were helpful and productive, and the other pile being all the thoughts you've had that were unhelpful and counterproductive, and assuming both piles were of approximately equal size, would more of the group of thoughts that emanated directly from your unconscious be in the helpful pile or more be in the unhelpful one?

And you go to the rendezvous with the other man, the man who shares your wife's bed when she is not with you, and he takes you to a large room full of people you somehow recognize. There are several well-known artists at the table as well as the man who once opened the door, who inquired about your idea 'which would contribute greatly to the secrecy and efficacy of the organization' and to whom you refused to tell anything. At this point in the dream you can barely recall how many years ago that was but are certain that you have noticeably aged since that time. And you are at a meeting where important things are being decided, important things for the future of the secret society and important things for the future of humanity. And you are having great difficulty following the exact meaning of the discussions since they are making reference to many things you don't know anything about or know about in only the vaguest of terms. Nonetheless, you are extremely excited to finally be at the centre of it all, where things are being discussed and decisions are being made. If only you could understand what the decisions being made actually pertained to.

So you start drinking, as you often do in uncomfortable situations, as you often do in dreams, and soon you realize you are extremely drunk. It is only this ridiculous drunkenness that allows you to stand up and make the following proposal:

"Hello everyone. This is my first time here. And I'm drunk." There is a smattering of amused applause at your drunkenness. "But I was thinking, I mean, I think that everyone here can't help but wonder why . . ."

No, of course you are not that drunk. There is probably not enough alcohol in the world to make you get up in front of a room full of strangers, strangers you respect and admire and for some reason wish desperately to be included among, and propose something chosen almost at random. However, that night you meet a couple and, because you are so drunk you cannot even remember where you live, they take you home with them. At first you think they are planning to propose sexual activities between the three of you but when you arrive at their home, a rather large modernist house overlooking a river, you realize that in fact they have something quite different in mind.

The last time I saw Paul was a little bit harrowing. I always felt that the main source of tension between Paul and myself was that Paul, consciously or not, resented the fact that I was a mildly successful mid-career artist while he, though he was clearly much more talented and brilliant than me, had no art career whatsoever and, to the best of my knowledge, had never produced anything or, at least, had never attempted to show anything or get published. And because I felt this way, and suspected that he had also felt this way for many years, in fact almost the entirety of the time I had known him, one night I decided to ask him about it. And it wasn't really like I was asking him anything, it was more like a direct confrontation, like I was accusing him of being a lifelong coward, accusing him of wanting to make and show art but being too afraid. He bristled at my accusation. "Artists are lepers," he said to me. "You, your friends, the entire world culture of artists and bohemians, it's like you have some strange sort of leprosy. All you want is people to look at you and look at what you do and think you're special and talented. You want it so badly that you think there's something wrong with those of us who don't." I nodded solemnly, feeling guilty as he continued, "Trust me, I don't need fan letters to tell me my thoughts are valid. I'm confident . . . My life has its own path . . . My thoughts are there own reward." And then he turned around and walked away, not looking back for even a second. I have to admit I didn't completely believe him. And of course now, when he passes by on his motorcycle and I try to flag him down, he no longer stops, just keeps driving.

In the living room the couple offer you green tea before revealing a secret panel in the wall, behind which sits a single book on a stand. The couple tell you the book is like a key to the secret society, it contains all its doctrines, strategies and histories. It was written by many people over many generations. The book is called *A Dream for the Future and a Dream for Now* and the moment you read the title you become aware of the fact that you are only dreaming and moments later you leave your own body, your own perspective, and enter into the bodies and perspectives of the couple whose home you are in. You enter both of them at the same time (don't ask me how this is possible) and you understand how they see you: They have let you into their home only to lead you astray, you are a nothing, a poser, some stray dog sniffing around the margins of their organization, and they are showing you the book only because it is a complete fake. The book is a broken map, a false lead they are providing only to distract you, to send you down wrong alleys in your misguided search to get closer to the heart of the organization. And then you are back in your own body, back in the part of the dream that is fully occupied by the character within the dream you identify as yourself, and you look at this couple who have invited you into their home, who have offered you green tea and hospitality and sympathy, but who have done so only because they feel scorn for you and wish to lead you astray. And all you are able to feel towards them is a delicate and infinite tenderness.

2. A Film that Will Make the Audience Feel Pure Joy

This is a film about a filmmaker who, while preparing to shoot her next project, one she has been working on for over twenty years, suddenly has a crisis of faith. (For the purposes of clarity we will refer to this individual as 'Filmmaker A.') Her crisis leads to a decision: She will take all the aspects of her upcoming film and, instead of shooting and editing them together, fully embody them within the patterns of her daily life. For example, if in her film Filmmaker A was planning a scene in which two close friends go skydiving, she would instead convince one of her closest friends to go skydiving with her. At first she thinks of such activities only as extended preparation for the eventual shoot but, over time, the idea of making the film is gradually replaced by this new idea of living it out instead.

At film school I was taught: A film has a protagonist and the protagonist has a goal and a well-made film sets as many believable obstacles as possible in the direct path of the protagonist (to make the audience feel all the more exhilarated when he finally does achieve his goal). The higher the stakes – in essence, the greater the eventual reward – the more desperately the protagonist will want to achieve his goal, the harder he will fight to overcome all of the humiliating obstacles the screenwriter so gleefully throws in his path. This standard formula somehow mirrors at least one aspect of the logic of capitalism, where the goal is to make as much money as possible, and all of the many things that get in the way of this ultimate objective must be steamrolled over like so many twigs in the path of a tank. People who work in film like to say that they are interested in storytelling, but I have found, on the whole, they are not. What they are interested in is the premeditated catharsis made possible when a certain kind of story delivers in a very specific way.

And as our film continues, as Filmmaker A pursues her newfound path, taking all the various aspects of her screenplay-in-progress and enacting them, weaving them effortlessly into the fabric of her daily life, it goes without saying that, rapidly, her life grows more dynamic, again and again becoming more active, more alive. Somehow, word spreads that this new strategy for 'filmmaking' is in fact infinitely more rich, productive and fulfilling than the previous, 'traditional' manner of working, and as word continues to spread, more and more films are replaced by their real-life embodiment.

Counterintuitive as such a concept might at first appear, audiences for these 'real-life cinema spectacles' also rapidly develop and grow. These audiences follow the exploits of the filmmakers solely through hearsay and rumour, since the authenticity of this 'filmmaking' is to be found in the fact that it is only ever lived, never filmed. However, even more than following rumours, these audiences are most easily identified by their tendency to imitate the logic and tactics of this newly emerging art form within the strictures of their own daily lives.

Within an ever-expanding milieu, 'filmmaking' becomes slang for scripting your life as if it were a movie, and then, throughout the process of such scripting, enacting quite naturally and casually each of the scenes you write. The avant-garde of this movement is to be found in those who choose to forgo the writing process altogether, simply living the film in real time, little by little, moment by moment, invisibly weaving it into their now considerably more compelling and immediate daily routines.

As you may or may not have already noticed, so far none of the characters in this film have names but I am about to introduce one that does. The character's name is Silvia. Because she has a name, and the others do not, naturally, possibly even against your better judgment, you will begin to identify with Silvia to a far greater degree than you have with any of the other characters mentioned so far.

Silvia meets Filmmaker A, and quite unexpectedly, they fall in love. Filmmaker A, being the founder of a movement, and what's more the founder of a movement that has had an enormous impact on the daily lives of its many participants, is much in demand as a speaker and workshop leader and therefore travels a great deal. Since new love is, more often than not, such a viscerally intense drug, she does not want to be separated from Silvia for even a moment and it feels quite natural for Silvia to travel alongside her.

Filmmaker A was scheduled to give a seminar at the film department of a university, and Silvia, as always, decided to accompany her. About forty students had gathered in the foyer, and they followed Filmmaker A out the front doors of the building and into the streets. "This is where the new filmmaking will take place," said Filmmaker A, as she gestured with her arms toward everything that surrounded them. "Without cameras, without actors. The film that is you and your engagement with the world that surrounds you."

The students followed and listened attentively, while Silvia hung back, keeping pace just a few feet behind. There were questions that Filmmaker A answered effortlessly, as if the questions had simply answered themselves, and she was only doing her best to keep out of the way. But from Silvia's perspective, standing slightly outside the group, what emerged was a different picture. The students were intrigued, perhaps even amused, but most of them remained completely unconvinced.

Then one of the students, a dark-haired girl with a sullen but mischievous smile, decided to make trouble.

"I have a question," the sullen girl said.

"All questions are welcome," Filmmaker A replied with a carefree wave, as if waving all questions towards her.

"These aren't really films you're making. You're just living your life . . ."

"Your definition of filmmaking is too narrow," Filmmaker A said. "That's what I'm here for: to propose another possibility, another way of seeing things."

"But you can't just call things whatever you want," the sullen girl continued. "I can't just say that's not a tree, it's a car, and if you disagree with me, accuse you of being too narrow."

"Of course if we change everything all at once – all trees are cars, all cats are birds – then it might be a bit confusing . . ." It was slightly off-putting how unfazed Filmmaker A seemed by this affront, which was clearly having an entertaining effect on the other students. "But things do change and can change.

Especially in the arts, there is an enormous potential for opening things up and re-evaluating our understanding of any given medium. A few hundred years ago, a urinal in a gallery wasn't considered art and yet now it's an essential part of the canon. And I propose that within film, we are now on the cusp of yet another one of these essential, liberating historical changes."

"But I still don't think a urinal placed in a gallery is art," the sullen girl replied.

"There are thousands of people in the art world who would disagree with you."

"The whole world could disagree with me. That doesn't make them right."

Filmmaker A paused and the entire group of students paused along with her. And it wasn't just her body that stopped moving. Suddenly her voice had slowed down as well, she was choosing her words more carefully now.

"I like you," she said, addressing the sullen girl directly, looking her straight in the eyes. "In a strange sort of way we agree. Perhaps most people in the world think that what I do isn't really filmmaking. But I don't care. I think it is and that history will prove me right. And who is there who can really decide the matter for good. No one. Each of us has to make up our own mind. I say it is. You say it isn't. Neither of us is going to look up in the sky one day and have the matter decided for us once and for all in fifty-foot high, flaming letters. We each have to decide for ourselves. All I ask is that you be open enough to hear me out."

The sullen girl smiled and met Filmmaker A's gaze a bit more directly than was polite.

"You're clever," the sullen girl said, smiling more and more as she continued. "More clever than I thought. I disagree with you and you respond by agreeing with me. That's good politics. But good politics aren't enough. The thing is I believe you, I believe that you're sincere, that you're living your fine, exciting life and really believe this great, dandy life you're leading should be referred to as filmmaking. I don't think you're insincere."

"Thank you," Filmmaker A said, ready to put the matter to rest and move on.

But the sullen girl wasn't finished: "The problem is . . ." she said, and by this point the entire group was hanging on her every word, "the problem is there is nothing more sad, more pathetic, than utter sincerity in the service of a lost cause."

Later that night, when Filmmaker A and Silvia were alone in their hotel room, and Filmmaker A had had a good cry and Silvia had done her best to console her (since Silvia wasn't really the consoling type), Filmmaker A was ready to put the whole unfortunate incident behind her. They were both getting ready for dinner, and Silvia, while Filmmaker A was zipping up the back of her dress, unthinkingly sent things spinning in the wrong direction.

"It was interesting what she said, though," Silvia said.

"You thought it was interesting," Filmmaker A replied.

"I'm not saying I agree with her," Silvia continued, trying her best to damage-control the oncoming flood. "Obviously I agree with you. And the way you handled the situation was spectacular."

"Then what . . ." Filmmaker A wasn't letting it drop, "What was interesting about it?"

"I don't know." Silvia was really searching now, searching for the door painted on the wall that would let her escape. "It's just if the whole world disagrees with you, and you still believe you're right . . . I mean, that's an interesting predicament."

Filmmaker A grabbed her bag and headed for the door. "You're an interesting predicament," she said, leaving the door slightly ajar behind her and yet, for a moment, Silvia was unsure whether or not to follow.

But dinner calmed everything down: spectacular food and a view overlooking the city. Everything was new enough that they couldn't stay mad at each other for long, and there was so much to talk about: the next day they were off to Vienna for another workshop and a few days after that the long journey to Tokyo, where a rather impressive series of events had been planned. Neither of them had ever been to Japan, and they talked about what it might be like – a cross between *Blade Runner* and *Lost in Translation* – laughing at themselves for how their points of reference were all from movies, and how appropriate and ironic it was that now – since Filmmaker A was in fact proposing that their life was a movie – they were imagining what lay in store for them as a series of movies they had already seen.

"Life in Japan is so cinematic already," Filmmaker A said. "It really feels like the perfect fit."

"Yes," Silvia said, trying to sound enthusiastic. But suddenly she found herself distracted, thinking about other things. Only a few months ago she had been living a completely sedentary life, heading to the office each morning, trying to push some films she had barely seen out into the world, so they might be barely seen by as many others as possible. And now that job, that life, felt a million miles away. New love was paying the bills. New art forms were replacing old ones, and the products of these new forms could no longer be distributed, had no room for the logic of publicity or opening weekends, could only be transmitted through word of mouth (which they always used to say was the best publicity anyway). And she had tethered her cart to these new forms, quit her job, politely severed old contacts and, with them, so many of her previous ways of seeing the world had fallen away as well. What if this sudden rush of pleasure, excitement, travel and yes, joy . . . what if it was only a momentary bump in the road? What if it didn't, or couldn't, last? Could she go back? Could she even bear the thought of returning to what, only a few months ago, had seemed to her a perfectly good, valid and enjoyable life?

"Are you all right?" Filmmaker A asked, watching her companion's mind wander but not knowing to where.

"Yes, I'm fine." Silvia did her best to snap back into the warm mood of the evening. "Just fantasizing about Tokyo."

"It's going to be delicious," Filmmaker A said.

"Yes," Silvia said, as they leaned across the table and kissed.

In Vienna there were official receptions so official they could barely believe they had been invited, much less been invited as the official guests of honour. In her talk to a room full of immaculately dressed Austrians, Filmmaker A stressed that her new mode of filmmaking was also a new way of living, a new way of seeing the world, and that new art forms, if they were to remain strong, mustn't emerge from a simple change in thinking but should instead develop out of a more fundamental change within life itself.

In the questions that followed, someone compared her work to that of the Actionists because she too was pushing her medium beyond what was previously acceptable. Even though Filmmaker A knew very little about Actionism, only that it had something to do with blood and shit, she agreed, continuing that cinema had in fact changed very little since D.W. Griffiths and Eisenstein first developed the basic vocabulary of wide shots and close-ups and Godard later added jump-cuts into the mix. Now it was time for a more substantial breakthrough.

Afterward some young people in attendance (Silvia wasn't quite sure but believed they were the children of the organizers) said they knew a place to go dancing and, on the way, handed out some pills, which Silvia and Filmmaker A washed down with long swigs from a flask of tequila covertly passed around the back of the taxi.

The nightclub was a huge concrete bunker, "Just like in a movie," Filmmaker A said, and they all laughed as the drugs kicked in. And the drugs themselves made everything more cinematic, slightly slurring their vision, framing the room in a series of rapid close-ups, while they danced and drank whatever was handed to them. The slurred, almost slow-motion, charge of their surroundings was intoxicating, and Silvia and Filmmaker A clasped each other clumsily, drunkenly kissing as the room spun and dancers jostled against them. They kissed and danced and kissed. "I think I'm going to be sick," Filmmaker A said, leaning into Silvia's ear, half-whispering and half-screaming to be heard over the music, as they stumbled rapidly toward a corridor they hoped contained a washroom, and Silvia pushed away the young people smoking cigarettes in front of the stall just in time, Filmmaker A now vomiting repeatedly into a dirty toilet, Silvia holding back her hair, continuing to comfort Filmmaker A as she washed out her mouth with water from the equally dirty sink. It wasn't long before they found a balcony where they could take in some air.

The music in the background was now like a faint memory, and Filmmaker A was sobering up a little but Silvia was still tripping wildly and started to talk as if talking were the only thing left to do with her life and the only thing that mattered: "What if our positions were reversed. I mean, what if you were me and I was you." Filmmaker A looked over at Silvia with bemused confusion as Silvia continued, "Do you know what I mean? If our positions were reversed, do you think you'd follow me around the same way I'm following you . . . ?"

"Of course I would," Filmmaker A tried to interject, but Silvia barely heard her.

"No," Silvia said, blindly throttling forward with the drug-fuelled velocity of her thoughts, as if her thoughts were leading the way and it was all she could do to keep up. "No, I don't think you would. I mean, because here's the thing, the obvious stupid thing that we never mention because it's too fucking obvious, but you, I mean you know this already, but you are really, really focused on your work. And then, and I'm not saying that I really mind, but then if I'm also focused on your work, we're both focused on the same thing and everything's fine. But if our positions were reversed, if I were focused on, let's say, my own work, whatever that might be, if I were to someday have my own work, then you'd still be focused on your work and we'd suddenly be travelling in two separate directions."

"What's this about?" Filmmaker A tried once again to interject, wanting to sound sympathetic but not sure where exactly to place her sympathy.

"What's this about . . . ?" Silvia was starting to get flustered now, her voice rising almost to anger, but a confused kind of anger, as if she herself could not quite understand what she was getting angry about. "It's about the fact that I'm looking around me, we're in Vienna and everything is great, and I'm looking around, and suddenly I start to realize that really I have nothing, do nothing, just follow you around like some sort of housewife or puppy dog."

"But I thought we were having fun." Filmmaker A was trying not to get upset, it certainly wouldn't help matters if they both got upset, blaming Silvia's outburst on the drugs, telling herself that in the morning everything would be better.

"Sure, we're having fun. You have a little groupie following you around the world, reinforcing what a great artist you are."

"Come on, Silvia, you know I don't think of you that way."

"No, of course not. I don't think of myself that way either. But this is where we are and this is what we're doing."

Silvia walked to the opposite edge of the balcony and started to cry, or maybe she was already crying. Filmmaker A was close behind and made an awkward attempt at an embrace, but Silvia pushed her away and stumbled back toward where they had been standing before. Now they were standing at opposite ends of the balcony and, for Silvia, the drugs starting to slow just a little; it was as if the music from inside was deafening, completely filling the space between them.

"If this was one of your projects, one of your films –" Silvia was really shouting now, trying to be heard over the music that was filling her head, trying to be heard over her own crying and anger, "if this was one of your projects then you'd really be paying attention. Then you'd know what the fuck I was talking about."

"What do you mean one of my projects?" Filmmaker A realized she couldn't help herself, she was getting angry, raising her voice too, as they stared each other down across the expanse of the warehouse balcony.

"One of your projects." Silvia was crying so hard now she could barely make herself heard. "One of your fucking projects. One of your films."

"What are you talking about?" Filmmaker A was really yelling now, really getting upset, "This is the film . . . What we're doing now, this is the film. Haven't you understood anything I've been saying . . ." But then she caught herself and quieted down a bit too suddenly, nonetheless continuing to speak, almost to herself, though still loud enough for Silvia to hear, "This is the film." Silvia was crying but listening. "This is the film. And it's heartbreaking. And it's wonderful."

3. Better Violence

Midsummer, stepping out onto my balcony. Hearing some re-
semblance to gunshots in the distance but thinking nothing of
it. The first sip of coffee is always the best, I think, smiling to
myself about the one-night stand who left just a few minutes
ago, left embarrassedly refusing breakfast therefore allowing
me this time alone, which is of course how I prefer it. I look
down, the street six floors below, perhaps hearing the same
gunshots again, this time closer. Then the gash of blood on the
wall behind me, turning to look at it with curiosity. The moment
in which I don't understand and then the next moment I do. It's
my own blood. I brush my hand against my temple, examine
the blood on my fingertips, look back down at the street.

They are far away but apparently close enough for a stray
bullet to have grazed me, and as they get closer I count four,
maybe five. Two are on scooters and the rest on foot, all being
chased by men in suits. (I naturally assume the men in suits are
cops.) Everyone has guns, and brief volleys of gunfire punctu-
ate the running. Against expectation, the mascots have the
bigger weapons. I count again, they are quite a bit closer, and

clearly there are five. The bear is in front, a rip across the chest through which half a breast is showing and another tear near the crotch where you can catch a bit of thigh. I stare at the bear leading the pack, machine gun in hand, perhaps thinking about her flesh just underneath the fur, in fact thinking about sex for a long moment until I notice the large, bloody gash in the back of her head, the costume smashed clear away, the bloodied head glaring through, blood matted and sticky, soaked into the small visible patch of blond, staining it blackish red. Maybe I am still thinking of sex, maybe you could fuck a gash like that, but as I am thinking my hand unconsciously rises to my own bloody forehead and I stop myself, wonder if I'm losing blood.

Behind the bear is a rabbit, an ice-cream cone, a tortoise and a kangaroo, all wearing the same tattered, furry outfits – cheap rental shit, the kind of thing from some second-rate children's show. Sawed-off shotguns and automatics held like they may or may not know how to use them and then they are gone. Several had been shot, fur gunked up and bloody, and I had been shot too so perhaps that is why I feel so 'on side.' Sympathy of some sort. I walk back into the living room, pick up the phone, call for an ambulance. After describing my injury in some detail they inform me that I am fine to drive to the hospital myself.

* * *

In the weeks that followed I thought a great deal about the incident. It of course might have been a hallucination, caused by the shock of the gunshot or too many drugs the night before, but I was certain it wasn't. I knew what hallucinations felt like, perhaps too well. This was clearly something else. What's more, as I so often do, I was considering making work about it, googling "furry," "mascot" and "guns," scrolling down through several pages of sex, sports and artillery before finally slipping across the following *Wikipedia* entry:

> Mascot Front is shadow organization, apparently underground, more or less impossible to track, possibly real, possibly apocryphal, focused on the social liberation of those who wear mascot uniforms (like those worn at sporting events) at all times, and wishing, while still wearing such uniforms, to have equal social and political status as all other citizens. Often violent, always inexplicable, their program is as ephemeral as their irregular, often unverifiable sightings and infractions.

I almost laughed out loud as I read this. But as I started to laugh my head hurt and I instinctively reached up to touch the spot where the bullet had nicked me. At the hospital they had wrapped the bandage too tightly. I continued to read:

> There is much speculation as to the origin and actual mandate of the Mascot Front. The predominant theory, sometimes referred to as the 'infraction conjecture,' posits a scenario in which, perhaps only as a prank or series of pranks, but perhaps also as an ongoing campaign, a number of Mascots were subject to a variety of infractions and persecutions at the hands of regional police including: 1) the tearing and soiling of mascot outfits, 2) sexual taunts, 3) capture and release in strange environments...

31

I stopped reading, my mind wandering elsewhere, realizing that I had in fact heard about all this once before, that when I had seen them that day on the street below, when the stray bullet had so effectively caught my attention, the scene already matched an image scratched into residual memory. Perhaps that was why I was not overly surprised at everything happening so quickly yet with all the familiarity of déjà vu.

* * *

Paul had a photograph he was endlessly fascinated by. I had no idea where he got it but I did know he kept it folded in his pocket, and by the time I saw it it was already quite faded and crumpled. The photograph showed four figures dressed in mascot costumes posing for the camera, each holding large machine guns at various angles. They were carefully poised, as if for a press photograph, and yet somehow it seemed that it wasn't simply a work of art (though viewing it as such was the most obvious interpretation) but in fact something quite different.

And then I asked Paul about it, trying to be precise, only to receive a series of vague, noncommittal answers as to its origin or how it came into his possession. What was clear, not in his words but in the enthusiasm he tried hard to suppress, was that this was simply one of his favourite things ever.

"You must know something. Come on, who are they?" I asked for the third or fourth time, knowing that in a moment I would have no choice, but still not quite wanting to let the matter drop. "What . . . it's from a party . . . friends of yours or . . . ?"

"Someday . . . maybe . . ." he said, in that state of thinking quietly to himself, but at the same time out loud, which was so often his manner, changing course mid-thought. "No, no . . . I have no idea who they are. I like the thought that sometimes rumours . . ." and then hesitating, half-changing course again: "That some rumours . . . feel true."

"Come on . . . I like it too. It's a great photo. Give me something here."

"We both know better than to believe in rumours." He smiled to himself, perhaps thinking that I in fact lived my entire life in a misguided mash of rumour and confusion. "No . . . just some moments. Moments of resistance. Moments of which no one precisely knows for sure. That's what we all want, don't you think, a mirage with the consistency of fact?"

I wanted to understand but I had no fucking idea what he was talking about. I looked down at the photograph again. He had been reluctant to show it to me. I had noticed it in his hand when he pulled it out along with his wallet to pay for the round. And now, when I reached out to touch it, he quickly refolded it, returning it to his pocket. At the time I thought little of the matter, only another of Paul's brilliant figments, the thoughts for which he should be internationally acclaimed but which, to the contrary, kept him mired in quiet obscurity. It was one of the many moments when I saw him more clearly, realized that he wanted no aspect of his situation to change, that his stubbornness was a map he would follow to the end.

* * *

A live encounter with the Mascot Front, preferably captured on video, would make a fantastic art project – the difficultly and

33

perseverance involved, the possibility for turning rumour into fact, and then later, fact into art (which would have the perverse side effect of throwing its factual status into question). The more I considered such aspects, as well as the basic novelty of the manoeuvre, the more I came to believe in the project's increasing potential to refine and further themes and strategies I had been developing throughout the entirety of my professional life.

Like most artists, my work had gone through the three basic stages: an early period of promise and energy, a middle period of strength, panache and consolidation, and finally a long period of semi-decline that appeared to have no beginning or end, in which all signifiers and trademarks of my practice remained firmly in place but any reason or authenticity behind the work felt increasingly scarce. For years I had been searching for strategies to fight this decline, strategies that involved no particular inspiration on my part but that instead could be generated through an in-depth analysis of my practice's current shortcomings. Yet I suspected such analysis was getting me nowhere, and what was needed was some sudden, desperate shift, a moment in which, perhaps only briefly, things might derail in order to stop repeating myself.

Not surprisingly, in and around such questions, I would often think of Paul, how he had put such struggles aside and instead succumbed to a pure, undiluted engagement with his own creativity. There could be no semi-decline because there was no work, only the purity of ideas he could apparently, indefinitely, turn round and round in his mind, contemplating them from every possible angle yet never committing to any form or path.

I had no leads yet I believed I could find them, or at the very least believed that the search itself could be contextualized as an artistic work and therefore, even if the trail ended in nothingness, such nothingness could itself become the thematic undertow of the work in question. I was aware of a certain degree of desperation in such a ploy but, upon further reflection, realized that desperation had served me well many times in the past and there was no reason to turn my nose up at it now. In his stubbornness Paul was utterly immune to such desperation, but I knew, had learned time and time again, that comparing myself to Paul would get me nowhere.

* * *

I had pulled the bullet out of the balcony wall and was going to gun shops, showing them the bullet, asking what kind of gun it might have come from and who sold such guns. I had a small camera crew with me, thinking the footage could eventually be of some use. The gun shop owners were, each in their own way, such fantastic characters. Stanley, who owned Sherbrooke Guns & Ammo, had a parrot he had taught to sing classic rock. We got a lot of footage of that bird. Elizabeth (Fine Weapons), with a little bit of persuasion, shot a quarter out of my hand. Moments before she did so I was thinking that if she shot my hand off we would definitely have something we could use. (Perhaps on a monitor directly beside the singing parrot.) In Sympathy for the Devil Small & Large Firearms, as I spoke with Samson – who had a tattoo of a small dog chewing on a very realistic rendering of a bloody human heart (the dog the tattoo was based on of course owned by his ex-wife) – there was a woman standing beside me at the counter. She had a very pleasant smile as she asked if it would be all right if we turned off the camera, she didn't like being filmed. I signalled for the cameraman to shut it off and, as we had previously agreed if such a situation should ever arise, he dropped the camera to his side but covertly kept rolling.

The woman was holding a duffel bag. I continued to ask Samson about his tattoo and ex-wife – his ex-wife who had in fact written an unpublished novel portraying Samson as leader of a satanic cult (the tattoo was his form of retaliation) – then showed him the bullet, watched him finger it carefully, and as he said, "I think maybe I sold this bullet," I glanced down at the duffel bag one more time (I had practically been staring at it for hours) and caught just the slightest glimpse of purple fur through a small, accidental opening in the zipper.

The woman with the pleasant smile was also looking at the bullet in Samson's hand, glancing over at me, glancing back at the bullet. I ripped a sheet of paper out of my notebook and quickly scribbled an improvised note, surreptitiously handing it to her. The note read: "I would like to interview you and your friends for an art project. Your anonymity is absolutely guaranteed. Art could be a valuable way to further your cause. I completely believe in what you are doing and find it inspiring." I then, perhaps a bit naively, included my address, email and phone number, and walked out of the shop high as a kite, absolutely unable to believe my good luck: a momentary coincidence and the project suddenly seemed feasible in a manner I had barely imagined possible.

* * *

Then, of course, nothing happened. I expected a phone call, an email, a letter – anything. At first, it seemed impossible to me that they would not jump at the opportunity to be part of a project by a fascinating and prominent internationally renowned artist. Then later, upon further consideration, long after the original thrill had worn off, it seemed impossible to me that I had been so naive as to think they would risk leaving the relative and anonymous safety of their covert existence for something as irrelevant and meagre as an art project. A strange thought would not leave my mind: most likely their lives were at stake. What reason had I possibly given them to entrust me with such a grave responsibility? And was it even a responsibility I desired? Was my desperation to invigorate my practice so intense that I was willing to potentially endanger the lives of others?

After a lengthy period of soul searching, of attempting to fully explore the ramifications of such questions – both for my own life and for the lives of the Mascot Front – I decided the only possible next move was to stake out Samson's shop. The term 'stake out' makes it sound like I had some idea what I was doing but of course I did not. I was simply imitating bad television shows about police, sitting in a nondescript rental car drinking coffee and pretending to read a newspaper, far enough away that I wouldn't seem too conspicuous, with the front door of the shop just barely in view if I craned my neck.

I sat there from nine to five for three straight weeks. Often in that spot I would think of Paul, of the folded-up photograph he perpetually kept in his pocket, which had perhaps been in his pocket for the entire time I knew him. I wondered where Paul was today, if attempting to track him down after all these years might be an even more personal and evocative project than this vague attempt to meet costume-wearing terrorists. I craned my neck and glanced over at the front door of Sympathy for the Devil Small & Large Firearms, straining to see if anything was active, for a moment thinking that the shop was not even open, when there was a rap on the window of the passenger side. I looked over to see Samson peering in on me. I rolled down the window, he asked to come in, I unlocked the door and he joined me. We sat in silence for a moment before he spoke:

"Just hanging out?"

"Meeting a friend a few blocks away. You know, had an hour or two to kill. Wasn't sure what to do with myself so ... thought I'd just pull over and read the paper."

"Sounds good."

A short awkward pause.

"Need a drive somewhere?"

"No. Got my motorcycle."

A long pause in which both of us looked straight ahead at the empty street.

"Can I ask you something?"

"Sure."

"This friend you're meeting. Were you also meeting them yesterday? The day before?"

An even longer pause, quite a bit longer, during which I considered lying. What kind of lie might be suitable in such a situation? It was extremely difficult to come up with something and I realized the longer I waited, the more insincere whatever I said next would appear. I decided to throw the dilemma back at him:

"What's your theory?"

"Don't know."

"Give it your best shot."

"You're an artist, right?"

"Yes."

"Contemporary sort of thing?"

"That's it."

"I think maybe sitting here in this car, drinking your coffee and reading the paper, might be part of some sort of art project. Is that right?"

"That's pretty good."

"Either that or you want to hook up with that girl?"

"Which girl?"

"The one in the shop. You handed her a note right?"

"Yeah . . ."

"She had a nice smile."

"It's true, she did. Do you know her?"

He chose his next words carefully.

"You don't want to . . . She's mixed up in some –"

As I interrupted a bit too suddenly:

"*That.*"

"What?"

"What she's mixed up in . . ."

"Yeah?"

"I want *that* to be my art project."

"Fucking hell."

"What do you think?"

He thought about it, was clearly thinking about it, but not for long before he pulled a gun out of his jacket pocket. It was a small gun. I thought maybe he was going to shoot me but instead he held it by the barrel and handed it over. I took it cautiously.

"It's not loaded."

"All right."

"Look at the handle."

I began to examine the handle, turning the gun over and around in my hands. Right at the bottom, etched into the part you might hit someone with if you were in a movie from the twenties, was a rather small drawing. I examined it more closely but remained unclear as to what it was of.

"It's a mascot."

"Yes."

"I'm not sure what kind. I think maybe a bear or dog . . ."

I examined it again. With his suggestion at the forefront of my mind, it did now appear to be a bear or a dog. It was a small etching, about half the size of a dime.

"Would you like to buy it?"

"I'm sorry."

"I sell guns, right?"

"Right."

"So I'm wondering if you'd like to buy it."

As I thought over everything that had happened the past month, pondering the purchase of both the gun and the small etching, another thought quietly occurred to me: I had never held a gun before. I wasn't particularly pacifistic but I was an artist and somehow the opportunity had never occurred. I placed the weapon's handle in my palm more firmly, trying to make the most of the opportunity, feeling its weight, sliding my finger naturally around the trigger.

"Careful."

"Why?"

"It's . . . loaded. A little bit loaded."

"I thought you said it wasn't."

"I just said that because, you know, I didn't want you to get any ideas."

"I'm not sure ... What kind of ideas?"

"Didn't want you to think of shooting me or maybe ..."

"Why the hell would I shoot you?"

"I don't know, you give a gun to a crazy artist and who knows what he might do."

I laughed at the idea of myself as a crazy artist.

"I'm not going to shoot you."

Samson seemed particularly pleased with this last statement. I handed him back the gun. We haggled over the price for a few minutes, finally agreeing on three hundred. I gave him the money and he handed me back the gun. It felt like we were passing a joint back and forth. As he was getting out of the car I wanted to ask more, search out another lead, but before I had a chance he was gone. I put the gun in the glove compartment, then worried I might forget it, might leave it there when I returned the car to the rental place, so instead moved it to my jacket pocket. It felt good against my rib cage as I drove home along the exact same route I had driven every evening for the past three weeks.

* * *

I bought a frame for the gun and hung it over my bed. Looking at it, over the course of many weeks, I realized I was unhappy with this form of exhibition. I therefore had a small box built. Five sides of the box were solid pine but on one side a circular hole had been cut. In this circle I placed a lens from the most

41

powerful magnifying glass I could find. I positioned the gun so that the etching was directly centred within the lens. Now I could see the etching more clearly, was amazed by the startling degree of detail, which I'll attempt to describe as follows:

The bear – for it is a bear, not a dog – is neither on all fours nor standing. It is like an animal in the process of becoming upright, facing the viewer, its curved back at a diagonal to the ground, as if it were raising itself up to attack or very rapidly evolving into a biped. In its paw is a gun, held tentatively yet firmly, identical to the one into which the engraving has been etched. The paw-held gun is about the size of a tick and yet rendered with such clarity as to leave no doubt that it is the exact same gun you are currently standing in front of. Looking more closely, in amazing detail considering the minute scale, it is possible to see a zipper running up the entire side of the creature, zipped all the way and ending just underneath the right ear. However, what is most amazing about this illustration is definitely the expression on the bear's face: a careful mixture of defiance and cunning. In a sense, it would be accurate to say the bear is simply grinning, but what a grin: subtle, sly, ready for a fight. Of course if the scale of the etching were more reasonable it is likely I would have been less impressed. But for me, drawn so minutely, that grin said it all: Anything is possible, do not underestimate us, we will surprise you, again and again, always when you are least expecting it.

Many nights before going to sleep I would stare at the etching for a few minutes, wondering about my project, what the next step might be, how to proceed. Of course, with the material I already had there were certainly things I could exhibit: the gun, the videos (including the video of a real-life Mascot Front member standing at the counter of a gun shop asking me to turn off the camera), the original bullet that had grazed me. But as a work it still felt unsatisfying. And then I would look at the etching again, such a remarkable and evocative degree of detail squeezed onto such a limited surface. Had anything I'd ever made been so concise or effective?

* * *

It was almost fall, some time around 2 or 3 a.m. I had been sleeping, had likely slept an hour or two, but then couldn't sleep, got up to take in some air on the balcony. The night was quiet and dead, more or less how I felt at that precise moment. I was thinking of taking a shower, heading out to some club, seeing if there were any young ones I could pull with my charm and résumé. Was I getting too old for this shit? More and more, as I entered, heading directly for the alcohol, feeling the volume and dissonance push into me, I would notice the women glance in my direction, dismissing me instantly, far more easily than they might have in the past.

The club was one possibility but there was also another. I had dug up some old notebooks a few days ago, they were sitting in a box on the kitchen table. Those notebooks had also thrown me into a nostalgic mood. There were about a dozen from the time when Paul and I saw each other most often. I had been going through them, half-systematically, mostly at random, looking for things Paul had said to me. I brought one of the notebooks out onto the balcony and was flipping though it absentmindedly, hoping that some thought or note might catch me unaware and spark something, some unexpected artistic possibility and then – the way it had happened so many times in the past – I would be off and running once again.

43

I had always found it productive to develop several projects at once and now, along with the Mascot Front, a project that had been in development for almost a year, I was considering a piece based on my recollections of Paul, wondering what form it might take, how I could make a viewer feel, or at least sense, all of the conflicted thoughts and feelings that had encompassed the dynamic between us. I knew, of course, that he would most certainly not approve of such an idea and so, concurrently, I also wondered if I could be confident that, if I were to go through with such an endeavour, he would never hear about it or see it. Or that if he did somehow chance upon it, and recognize himself (since I was most likely planning to use 'Paul' instead of his real name and alter key details of his story to preserve his anonymity) there would be no particularly gruelling repercussions. The art world remained marginal, one could generally feel confident that statements made within it would not reach those who were outside. But then again, what did I know of Paul's life now, perhaps he had changed course: become an art critic or curator, would show up at the opening and glare at me from the corner with that look of withering disgust he had all but perfected at the time during which I still knew him.

Thinking about it, imagining this extremely unlikely fantasy scenario, I realized how his imagined glare would fill me with such a deep sense of shame, such a deep sense of self-loathing, that I am unsure how I would handle it. And then I thought about it all again and suddenly the idea of Paul as an art critic or curator felt so completely ridiculous I almost laughed out loud. Suddenly I felt good again, gazing out at the city, pockets of electric light surrounded by larger pockets of extended

44

darkness, almost laughing out loud at my own preposterous thought.

I looked down at the notebook in front of me. There were a series of statements that Paul had made, written down after-wards in the best half-remembered approximation I could muster, each sentence or series of sentences with a circle or box around it. And staring down at the notebook page, at all the boxes and circles, I felt near bafflement at my former self. I had never been a fan. How did Paul manage to hook me like that? But of course the answer was obvious, because the way he lived and thought was like a battering ram upon my key insecurity: that as an artist I was an impostor, a sham, that my work was only pumped up strategy and cleverness. That if you scratched away at it hard enough, underneath there was nothing, no truth or authenticity, no sincerity or vision.

As I thought this, instinctively – I'm still not quite sure why – I half-turned towards the kitchen and at that same moment heard a sound, a small crash as if someone had knocked over a chair or table, and I stepped inside just as a bear mascot and a blue popsicle mascot were stepping out of my bedroom. How they had managed to get into the apartment so quietly I had absolutely no idea. The box with the gun was under the Pop-sicle's arm, and as he turned to look at me he seemed almost startled, as if up until that moment he had assumed he was alone in the apartment, while it felt rather obvious to me that I should have been the one to be startled, surprised at the degree to which I was not, calm and assured, as if a bear and popsicle stealing back their etched pistol was the most natural thing in the world.

And before I had even managed to take a second step into the

45

kitchen the Bear was already on top of me – I couldn't believe how fast she was able to move in that oversized suit – then a smash across my face as I began to fall, a sheet or bag wrapped over my head as I was going down and my wrists behind my back being held or tied, yet I didn't feel alarmed, only surprised and impressed at the incredible efficiency and speed at which it was all happening. I could feel my body being picked up like a sack, the bruises on my back, neck and legs as they hauled me into the elevator, moments later throwing me into the trunk of what I assumed was a van or a car. Throughout all of this I didn't try to resist. I was getting what I wanted: a live encounter with the Mascot Front. In one sense or another they had received my note. I could hear an engine revving, feel the streets passing outside, all the while seeing nothing.

4. A Dream for the Future and a Dream for Now

Paul and Silvia weren't really a couple.

"It wasn't the part with Hitler ass-fucking the dog that pissed me off..." she said.

Or Paul and Silvia were a couple but when people asked they (usually) said they weren't.

"Then what?" They were arguing but it wasn't so bad. He'd seen worse.

"It was because you went to such great lengths to describe how much the dog enjoyed it."

Or Paul and Silvia were neither a couple nor not a couple, but lived together and fucked occasionally yet never thought of each other as partners, only as creatures who had hopped onto the same train for a short while and now found themselves temporarily along for the ride.

"But that's what makes it funny."

A new book was a new book, stories stitched together and sent out into the world. There would be readings, reviews, reviews that made him happy (good days) and reviews that made him angry (bad days).

"I get that it's supposed to be funny," she didn't even know why she was arguing, his books were his books, he should be free to write whatever the fuck he wanted, his books were *not* their relationship, which was confusing enough as it was, she should know better than to confuse the two, "and I get that it's supposed to be funny because it's not what we're expecting, we don't expect the dog to enjoy it quite so much. But what you don't get is that underneath all your presumed subversion is the same business-as-usual macho control-freak cruelty that we've been drowning in practically forever: 'Not only am I going to fuck you over but I want you to enjoy it too.'"

He wanted to respond but he didn't. He wanted to sulk but he didn't want to give her the satisfaction. He hated being called macho.

"Sure, you can call me macho, a control freak . . . whatever . . ." He was stumbling for words, he hated it when the words didn't come naturally. "You know I hate being called macho, I hate . . ." If he could have slapped her he would have but he had never slapped anyone in his life and in fact had never even considered it and didn't know why the fuck he was considering it now. "I hate . . . fuck . . . We both know this shit."

"What?"

"In real life . . . fuck . . . In real life . . . I . . . fuck . . ." He just wanted the discussion to be over, he just wanted to spit out what he had to say and then for the conversation to fucking end: "In real life I'm not cruel." It was ridiculous to hear him say it. Of course they weren't talking about real life. Of course he wasn't cruel.

But his book was.

* * *

48

Silvia was also working on a book. The working title for her book was *A Dream for the Future and a Dream for Now*. She hated that title. But she had already agreed to it eighteen years ago and she was fucked if she wasn't going to keep her word.

In her book a secret society who went underground just after World War One has resurfaced in late-forties New York. They are staging large-scale orgies in order to assassinate prominent businessmen by infecting them with a contagious disease efficiently designed so that anyone with a genuinely leftist or humanitarian outlook will remain permanently immune. Some of the members in the sect are involved in order to further the revolution while others are there only because they want to participate in as many orgies as possible.

The book begins when a woman – who most of the time appears to be a stand-in for the author – attends one of the orgies and catches the virus (allegedly designed to attack only the Right). Since she has always been confident in her defiant political radicalism she is faced with a dilemma: Either the virus is defective or she's not as leftist as she confidently assumed.

At the orgy she meets a man and they fall in love. The man turns out to be a woman masquerading as a man but our protagonist doesn't care, man or woman it doesn't matter, because mainly she wants to have as much sex as possible before she succumbs to the disease (which she still feels she shouldn't have caught in the first place). Our protagonist and her new love fuck in many different places and each time it is like a knife in each of their hearts because they both know she will die and the reason she will die is the same reason they first met.

Secretly Silvia thought her book was much better than Paul's – more anarchic, more original, more alive, more subversive.

Paul knew she thought this, so it wasn't actually a secret but rather an unspoken tension between them. Paul felt that even if her book was better, his book would be more successful because the publishing structures surrounding literature remained essentially chauvinistic. This fact made him both confident in the potential for his own book and sad the world wasn't a more reasonable and fair place.

* * *

That night in the car, on their way to dinner, Silvia felt increasingly anxious. She knew she would have to suffer the entire drive in silence. When Paul shut down like this there was little she could do to bring him out into the open. In a few days he would come out on his own, buy her a present, meekly apologize, claiming to be too sensitive, too much of an artist for his own good, things would slowly drift back towards normal, and she would know better than to criticize his work again any time soon. What's more, what made her feel truly awful, as the twilight grey scenery sped past unwatched, was the realization that, if she were to view the matter with a certain distance, she had in fact only criticized his book in order to procrastinate, to distract herself from having to fully commit to finishing her own. She hated these tepid patterns. Time and time again falling into the exact same traps, avoiding what was really important only to rush headlong into the same tedious snag.

She looked up from her thoughts and realized they were already pulling into the driveway. Now she knew the drill, time to push the real feelings down into the bottom of her stomach, be friendly, sweet, clever and charming, a good partner to Paul (always keeping in mind that their model remained unconventional, that at the end of the day they weren't actually a couple) and a strong, confident writer in her own right.

At the door they were greeted with hugs and kisses and a display of basic human warmth she was afraid they simply could not match. But despite her nervousness, they were now among friends and definitely not on trial for being a bad couple or bad people, and any flaws that may or may not be on display were to be blithely overlooked in favour of an almost complete sense of acceptance.

* * *

Jeremy and Theresa lived in a crisp modernist house overlooking the ravine. They had moved there just a few months ago, after life had decimated in L.A. and they suddenly found themselves needing refuge from the harsher aspects of their professions. In the course of just two short years attempting to cut through the blockade of the industry, they had lost energy, become fragile, even paranoid. Having set out for acclaim with potential to burn they had now returned with little hope they would ever catch fire again. But what was strange, and perhaps even unnerving, was how relaxed they seemed in their shattered, potential paranoia. Years of working the system had lent them a friendly, cordial air that made everything they touched feel welcome and loved.

Paul and Silvia felt especially loved. Neither of them had ever gone for easy money, or been seduced by the blatant rush of media glamour, and evidence of their newfound friends' initial promise, but eventual failure, to achieve such things made them feel a strange confidence in their own chosen paths, and in opportunities for their advice to be both useful and cherished:

Paul: I'd be satisfied if the new book only appeals to a few –

Silvia: You don't know that yet. You have no idea how many people may or may not like it.

Jeremy: I couldn't see the point of doing something if I didn't feel as many people as possible would be –

Theresa: You say that but, come on, you're too stubborn. You don't exactly make concessions.

Paul: He's just confident that what he likes will also be liked by a lot of other –

Silvia: I'm surprised if even Paul likes what I write much less –

Jeremy: Of course Paul likes what you –

Theresa: No, I'm insecure too. If a friend tells me they thought my last thing was strong I'm virtually in shock for a –

Paul: I can't believe how consistent it is. All my male friends, no matter how mediocre their work, always think they're God's gift to art. And all the women, no matter how brilliant, are completely insecure.

Silvia: Is that really true?

Jeremy: Of course.

Theresa: It just seems that way to you because women are more open with how they –

Paul: It doesn't just seem that way. It's really like that. I don't want to speculate on reasons but –

Silvia: Boys and girls are just raised differently. Boys are praised for being clever and asserting themselves. Girls are praised for being pretty and quiet and –

Jeremy: Yes, but –

Theresa: You don't know what you're talking about. No matter what else has happened you've always managed to catch a break.

Paul: 'Always' seems like a bit of an –

Silvia shot Paul a look. The look suggested he might be crossing a line he shouldn't. Everyone knew that in L.A. 'catching a break' was furthest from what happened.

Jeremy: It's all right. You win a few, you –

Theresa: Sometimes I worry we're only pretending . . . I mean no, not pretending . . . I mean, of course, well, pretending . . . pretending is too strong, I mean of course things are all right: great house, great friends . . . But, no, I mean, no, no . . . I don't know . . .

After dinner, in the living room over coffee and cognac, Jeremy and Theresa drew quiet for a time, shooting each other awkward, conspiratorial glances. Paul and Silvia waited patiently. From the tone of the room it seemed evident that something was about to happen, or perhaps they had only offended their hosts and this awkwardness was the sign they should now leave.

"We have something to show you," Jeremy finally said, then walked across the room, pressed a panel in the wall and, like in some bad movie, a small secret compartment opened at about face level, just the right size to house a single, hardcover book. It was unclear exactly what kind of book it was and yet at the same time everyone could clearly read the title: *A Dream for the Future and a Dream for Now.*

Paul looked over at Silvia, for a moment questioning the accuracy of his own memory: "Isn't that the title of the book you're working on?"

And Silvia is seventeen and out with three of her closest friends. In fact they are her only close friends. They go out practically every night together. They are drunk and stoned, like many other nights, like most nights, wandering the streets, saying anything and everything they can to stave off the boredom or generate a bit of spark. Almost dawn and wandering down the grey streets near the mall, kicking around a stolen shopping cart and laughing, stupidly, for no reason, every time it topples or lurches forward.

"No, I'm going to write a book and it's going to be really long, longer than the Bible, and it's going to be sharp, sharp enough to cut yourself . . ."

"What's it going to be about?"

"My book's going to be twice as good as your book."

"Fuck off."

"When did you get so competitive?"

"I'm never competitive. I just like to state the facts."

"It's going to be about my life. But not my life the way it is now or the way it will be then. About my life all the different ways it could have been if I could have made every single decision that was possible to make. Because most times, you have to decide, like, do I go to law school or do I go to art school. But my book will be like if you could split in two, but still be just one person, and go to law school and art school at the same time and see them both through to the very end. And like that with everything, what if you could do all the things, never having to choose, and all the options you've done and are doing would all exist at the same time. That's why it's going to be so long."

"I'd like to write a biography some day."

"You think your life is going to be so interesting?"

"It doesn't matter if your life is interesting. It would just be worth it to get it all down. Let other people decide whether it's worth reading."

"We should all write biographies. In twenty years. We all write biographies and meet here again to find out what we've all done with our stupid lives."

"I'm in."

"What if we all wrote books with the exact same title . . ."

"What?"

"They wouldn't even have to be biographies. In twenty years, twenty years from today . . . fuck, this is really brilliant."

"You're stoned."

"I'm definitely stoned. But come on, who's in? In twenty years, whatever else we're doing, we each write a book with the exact same title. That would really confuse things, four books with absolutely nothing in common, unrelated, in different parts of the world, all being published with the exact same title on the exact same day."

"That's ridiculous."

"You're ridiculous. This is fucking brilliant." ·

"I'm in."

"None of us are even going to remember this in twenty years."

"We will if we make a pact."

Over the years that followed, the pact became a kind of endless, ongoing joke, with many discussions and arguments as to what 'the title' should be – the title that all four of their books would eventually share, with prominent contenders including: *Not Enough and Too Much*; *Sublime Resistance*; *With My Best Work Behind Me*; *Almost Happiness* and *I Had Meant to Fail*. As is often the case in collective decision-making, the final result landed somewhere that no one was completely happy with. Still, a few years of discussing the pact (at first mainly as a joke, yet over time becoming a joke, and later an idea that was increasingly important to them) gave the title an aura that gradually began to feel useful and even inevitable.

* * *

"Of course that's the title of the book I'm working on." Silvia glanced over at Paul, unsure, under the circumstances, whether

56

to express amusement or exasperation. "You don't know the title of my book?" And yet the last thing in the world she wanted was to express any sort of exasperation or frustration in these kind and relaxed circumstances. Kind and relaxed was true. But as they all sat there staring at the book propped up behind the once hidden and now open panel, she had to admit that far more than 'kind and relaxed' the circumstances were mainly, perhaps even overwhelmingly, uncanny.

"I mean, I know that's the title of your book, but . . ." Paul started to laugh. "I mean, I just meant that it makes no sense. For them both to have the same title."

This wasn't the reaction Jeremy and Theresa were hoping for or expecting. This book was easily their most cherished object, patiently at the centre of all the very best aspects of their new life together. It had opened up for them a way of living that was completely new, contrary to all of their previously held assumptions about what was and was not possible, filled with delicious new possibilities for life and work. How could it have the same title as a book their friend Silvia was also writing? What kind of coincidence was this and how could they integrate this new information into all of the other discoveries the cherished book had helped them make so far?

"We wanted to tell you about this book," said Jeremy, unsure whether what had just happened should in some way alter their original plan, "because we think this book . . ."

Theresa picked up the thought: ". . . we think this book has a potential to . . . the potential . . ." But she couldn't go through with it. It was all too strange. She found herself at a complete loss for words.

* * *

After they got home, when Paul had gone up to bed alone, Silvia sat down at her computer and began to write:

She walked into the orgy with her head held high. They had decided to meet here, like they had met the first time, and she wanted to seduce and devour every last moment, make every moment as delicious as the first. She stepped over two naked boys who were entangled with the CEO of some right-wing think tank the name of which currently slipped her mind, his suit jacket and tie dishevelled but still more or less on, his cock being sucked by one boy while the other pressed up against his ass. Soon he'll have the virus, she thought. Soon he'll be just like me. Just overhead two large cages swung gently back and forth, the naked bodies in configurations that made it difficult to ascertain how many were in each: the slow, gentle fucking and stroking just enough to keep the cages in constant, vertiginous movement.

Across the room she spotted him, in the same mask and cape as before. She moved forward through the naked, entangled bodies, tracing a semicircle across the room, moving steadily towards him. She remembered the first time she had done this, not sure why she was drawn there, spontaneously pressing her face against the mask. Maybe it was the mask itself, something you could press your face against that would not give or kiss back. And how as she had pressed her face against the mask a hand slid up her skirt, not all the way, content to lightly stroke the soft flesh of her inner thighs. They had said nothing that night, fucking in the corner over and over again. And she remembered being perplexed at the way the strap-on he was using as a cock felt inside, thinking she had never felt a cock quite like that before, but she still had no idea what was underneath the mask and that night she barely cared.

Once again she pressed her face against the mask. Once again that hand, a hand that belonged to a woman she now loved almost more than her own life, slid up her skirt and gently stroked her inner thigh. Their faces were so close and yet separated by a thin layer of hard plastic. She could feel the heat of her lover's face through the barrier, smell and almost taste the sweat as her teeth gently pressed against the mask, almost biting, almost chewing, as she had done before, as the anticipation continued to grow, becoming almost too much to bear. Hand in hand they slid over to that same dark corner, pressed up against the wall and then tumbling down onto the floor. Unlike before, she now felt under the cape for a nipple, pinching it, twisting it through the stiff fabric of his button-down shirt. Now she knew how much her lover wanted this, back then she had not.

It was dawn by the time they left together, hand in hand, drenched in sweat and every kind of fluid. They walked all morning, finally stopping at the water where the sun was already bright and sharp and low in the sky, straining their sleep-deprived eyes as they curled up together with their feet hanging over the edge of the pier. She had never felt better and realized that even though she was terrified of the weeks and months to come – even though she had no dreams of facing death bravely and knew she would bend and crumple into desperate sadness and ache as the virus progressively took its toll – she had spent these last weeks well. She had found love and fulfilled it with all of her being. She had taken risks. And, however misguidedly or ineffectively, she had fought against power. Death would not take any of that away from her.

Silvia paused at this last line. Paul would never write a line like that, he'd consider it only pretentious and vague. Silvia didn't mind the occasional, evocative vagueness and was not afraid of pretension. But the line bothered her anyway: "Death would not take any of that away from her." It was mystical. She had never been mystical. And then Silvia thought back to the book behind the panel. She'd had a perfectly reasonable explanation for the coincidence but had kept it to herself, preferring that everyone else in the room remained in the grip of its strange, uncanny mystery. Why had she done so, why hadn't she explained? She put such thoughts momentarily aside, put her hands on the keyboard, and continued to type:

Sitting on that pier, kissing for awhile and, from time to time, drifting for a few moments in and out of sleep, as the sun slid up over the water and into the sky, she felt that life was boldly opening up for her while at the same time it was violently shutting down, and everything felt great and alive and charmed and hopelessly unfair.

They went back to her place, showered together

sleepily, the hot water washing away all signs of the orgy as they held each other tightly, falling into bed and into a sleep so deep it was as if all dreams and reality for a single moment ceased to exist, their naked, sleeping bodies completely entwined. They had slept like this often, face to face, legs interlocked, arms holding on for dear life, as if they were two pieces of a jigsaw puzzle that, once placed together, completely made sense and, if taken apart, could never make as much sense or fit as smoothly with anyone or anything else.

* * *

After their guests had left, Jeremy and Theresa felt little more than dejected. They had been planning their presentation for weeks and to see it cut off so suddenly and strangely was a hangover they really didn't need after all of the hangovers and disappointments of the past year. They knew that if only more people would simply read the book, if they could introduce them to its many wonders and pleasures, something startling would gradually become possible – not only for them, though they would certainly not be ashamed to accrue all possible benefit from the book's dissemination, but more importantly for each and every person they managed to convince.

* * *

Paul couldn't believe Hitler had once again made an appearance in his new book. He had promised himself he would never write about Nazis again. It was such a blindingly ineffective trope. Every third-rate first novel you picked up took place during World War Two, or had some character who had survived World War Two, or a character with a mysterious Nazi past. And yet seemingly he couldn't help it. His feather-light Jewish education, which he had sat through begrudgingly, and believed at the time he was successfully ignoring, had obviously contaminated the groundwater of his imagination, and though he could barely remember the names of any High Holy Days, and most certainly could not tell which was which, when he wrote literature Nazis would continuously appear, and he would just as rapidly try to cut them out, edit them away, as if he was fighting his own personal, literary underground resistance. Except with this resistance, each and every time, he was both the Nazi and the resistance fighter, everything spinning up and around within the free play of his imagination. To give himself rules was of little help: a simple rule such as 'no Nazis' – it seemed he couldn't even follow that.

Because here was the thing: When you were an artist, at least within the work, you always got praise for pushing things too far. And for Paul, pushing too far generally seemed to involve bringing a few Nazis into play. He wandered downstairs and stood in the warm light of the kitchen. He examined the espresso machine, turning it on as he did so, checking if there was still enough water. It was early and Silvia was asleep. She liked to write late into the night while he preferred to write in the mornings. He slipped in a cup and listened to the coffee grind. The smell of espresso already made him feel happy, and he walked over to the window, stared into the sunshine. It was a bright beautiful day, and there were no Nazis in his life, in fact no real unpleasantries or dangers of any kind. There were some occasional money problems, but that was only normal when you were an artist. He walked back over to the machine, took the cup and first sip, then walked over to the table and sat down.

Silvia's computer was still open on the kitchen table. He pressed the space bar to awaken the screen, then hit save, just in case she had forgotten to save her work the previous night, as she sometimes forgot to do when the exhaustion of her late-night writing sessions slowly wound her down. He paused before he began to read. Would she mind if he examined her work-in-progress, uninvited and without prompting? They usually showed each other the books they were working on. In fact, showing her his own final chapter had recently been the cause of their last big fight. Nonetheless he began:

She wasn't sure how she knew it would be her last morn-ing on earth but somehow she knew. They woke up, as always, completely intertwined. The sun was bright through the window. It felt good to be in love.

He paused at this sentence. Was he in love with Silvia? Did it feel good? He thought about it for a brief moment and realized that clearly he was and it did.

It felt good to be in love and yet suddenly she knew what must be done. She silently slipped out of the embrace, took her clothes into the next room in order to dress with-out waking her lover, and slid out the front door just as quietly, out onto the street down which she strode with greater and greater confidence.

Headquarters was not far away and there were several

men there, each clearly deserving the full fury of her retribution. Yet there was one she felt certain was worse. He was the architect of so many catastrophes, taking huge sums of money and, like some evil alchemist, transmuting it directly into blood. The things he had bought and sold: people, lives, nations, companies and of course also works of art. There were so many just like him, but in her memory he alone took such a peculiar pleasure in profiting from the many disasters he generated, using a method that could only be described as half-accident, half-Machiavelli. (But were the accidents really accidental or were they only put in place to obscure how purely Machiavellian his strategies actually were?)

She remembered him, and as she did there was one particular memory that lashed back at her more precisely than the rest, from a time many years ago (before she'd joined the resistance). Back then she was still working for the company, had not yet realized how impossibly wrong this situation was, had not yet set herself the task of working towards its destruction, towards undermining every last inch and thrust of its values and program. And she was working with him, he was her boss. Day after day she saw at such close distance exactly how he operated.

In this particular memory she was at her desk. She looked up. She saw him at the far side of the open-concept office. He was leaving. It was mid-afternoon on a Tuesday, so there was no reason for him to leave, but he looked distressed. There were a few things she had to discuss with him, work matters it would be best to clear up before the end of the day, and she thought maybe she could catch him in the elevator or stairwell. She stood up. Yet as she was doing so she realized that the things she had to ask him were actually not so important, not the real reason she was standing up, not the real reason she was following him into the staircase, out the front doors of the building, down the street. In fact, of course, it was curiosity that was driving her, curiosity about that strange (she even remembered thinking, at the time, mean-spirited) look on his face, curiosity about what possible reason he might have for leaving the office half-way through the afternoon.

And the next thing that was strange, that peaked her curiosity even further, was that instead of heading into the parking garage and getting into one of his many cars, he walked two blocks north before descending into the subway. She was not sure she was at a correct distance to follow without being spotted, but even more urgently she was afraid of losing him. Why was she afraid of losing him? She realized how desperately she wanted to see some other side of his life, to feel her suspicions con-firmed, or to see that such suspicions were little more than paranoid ghosts and in such a manner put them out of her mind once and for all. As she followed she made up stories of what she might say if he turned and spotted her. That she was on her way to a doctor's appointment or that her mother had been rushed to the hospital. (But then why wasn't she taking a taxi? But then again, why wasn't he taking one of his many cars?) She got into the subway along with him, in the next car, trying to keep him in view and remain out of sight.

Up out of the subway, she was one block behind him as he strode down the street at a pace she found difficult to match. He turned into a doorway and, not sure whether or not to follow, she crossed the street to watch, further assess. It was a building, she couldn't tell whether it consisted of offices or apartments, about five floors, nondescript. There were likely many rooms in such a building and if she entered she considered how long it might take to find him, and what she would do if she actually did. But she didn't have to think for long, as moments later her boss came storming back out. If he had been paying attention he would have seen her, standing across the street in clear daylight, staring straight at him in utter disbelief. Yet the source of his preoccupation was not difficult to ascertain. He was wiping blood, a great deal of blood, off of his hands with a white handkerchief.

Paul paused. It was scenes like these that irked him most within the world of her writing: the sledgehammer of didactic yet ironic obviousness. In the real world nothing was like that: one would never catch the evil CEO with literal 'blood' on his hands. They always found others to do their dirty work, usually others who were as far away as possible, others they could not in any way be connected to in a court of law.

And yet he reminded himself that, at the same time, it was also what he liked most about her work. That it spoke so little about real life, about how things really were, but instead was always a fable of power, sex and imagination and how we are often much too afraid of being literal.

She remembered that blood and that handkerchief and the strangely blank expression on her boss's face as she continued to speed towards headquarters, as she walked through the front doors of the building and past the security guard, who for a moment thought to stop her but then, moments later, when she was already gone, decided to let it pass. She went up towards the twenty-eighth floor, across the expanse of the open-concept office, past his secretary who also tried to stop her at the same time smiling in recognition as she pushed past. Into the office, where he stood in the corner on the phone. He put his hand over the receiver and looked straight at her.

"I want to fuck you on your desk," she said. She would give him the virus and then she would die. And afterwards he would die. Which was of course the point.

* * *

Jeremy and Theresa had locked every door in the house and shut off all the lights, except the one in the bedroom, when they heard the crash, violent, like a large tree had fallen in a storm, smashing into the back wall of their crisp modernist house. But there was no storm. And it wasn't the first time they had been startled in such a manner.

"Do we go look now? Or wait until morning?"

He was trying to remain calm, thinking nothing could be gained by taking an already tense situation and adding panic to the equation.

"I won't be able to sleep if I don't know."

"You might not be able to sleep if you do."

"It can't be any worse that the last one." But as she said this she also feared that maybe it could. That what could definitely get worse was their fear of never extricating themselves from such a tangle, that eventually they might turn against each other and that would really be the end.

This was the real reason they had left L.A., though apart from the occasional outbreaks of reheated paranoia, most of the time they managed to convince themselves, and each other, that the reason they had fled L.A. was their inability to build on their initial promise to achieve anything resembling real success. But these incidents were a painful reminder of the reality just underneath their half-invented cover story, of how bad things had actually gotten in the months and weeks before they finally decided to flee.

As they walked down the staircase towards the back garden, Theresa could sense Jeremy's entire body tensing. Flicking each light back on as they passed, Jeremy wondered how it had gotten so out of hand, wondered what might have happened if they had never discovered the book, or if it had never interested them, or (at the very least) if they had never become so involved.

There was a floodlight that covered the entirety of the back garden, and Theresa's hand paused just in front of the switch, as if what remained in darkness, what remained unknown, also remained innocuous. Did she really want to flick the switch and see further evidence that they weren't welcome here either, that their relationship with the others had deteriorated beyond repair? But of course the switch was flicked and the floodlight went on.

What they saw was as predictable as it was unnerving. The

entire back wall of the house had been covered in blood. It was difficult to imagine how so much blood could have splattered so completely.

"What will we do?"

"I'll get the hose."

* * *

When Silvia finally came down for breakfast Paul was still at the kitchen table, still reading, a smile on his face as he gradually teased through the story of the assassin and her boss, how they had been lovers when she worked for him, how it was in the bedroom she had first learned just how savagely he approached his work, how for him a dollar earned was all that much sweeter if earned at the expense of someone else. And then the turning point when she joins the resistance, becomes a double agent, realizes she can use the bedroom to gather information, gather whatever details he would casually drop, test the limits of how much she could safely pry, until one day, as far as her boss was concerned, she simply disappears – all of these memories rushing through her mind as she fucks her boss to death on his desk in that corner office on the twenty-eighth floor.

"This is fantastic," Paul said.

Silvia was at the espresso machine. She wondered whether or not to believe him. Was he just making nice, trying to patch things up from their big fight the night before?

"What's so fantastic about it?"

And then the pause, the pause that was a few moments too long, the pause, the opening, during which all of her insecurities about her work, about life, came flooding through.

"I don't know..."

The pause followed by an 'I don't know,' as if he was buying himself time, fishing for something to say, something convincing, something that would convince her that he thought her work was strong and therefore be the first step towards assuaging the tensions of the night before.

"I like the way it rushes forward, steams through the clichés, almost breaking them open as it goes."

She focused on the word 'cliché,' on the word 'almost,' how he doesn't say it breaks open the clichés but that it 'almost' does, how he perhaps doesn't think her writing is good at all, but only 'almost' good. She pulled the espresso cup from the machine, leaned against the counter with her shoulder facing him, taking the first morning sip.

Paul could see that something had gone horribly wrong, that whatever he said next would most likely hurtle towards another fight. He felt trapped. Trapped in his role as the one who's always too critical, who always judges her harshly, who, when it comes to books, can't help but be competitive, who after all these years together, couple or not, had never found the right way to be on her side.

"I said your book was fantastic."

"Yes."

"And now you seem angry."

"Yes."

"I'm lost... What do we do?"

She looked at him. He did look genuinely lost. She also felt lost. They were both writing books. He was almost finished his. She still had a long way to go.

"If we're not a couple, why do we always act this way?"

The wall was clean, the blood washed away. Jeremy and Theresa lay in bed, thinking, unable to sleep. They loved the book, but the other people who loved the book clearly did not love them. They hadn't meant to make anyone angry. It just seemed so clear to them that there was a certain, very specific, way the book should be shared. And that this way was extremely different from the manner in which the others were teaching it. That people should come to the book gradually, gently, based on their own initiative, with few or no strings attached. That money and the secrets of the book should be kept separate, at least at first. The small gatherings they had in their home, during which they introduced a few close friends to the book, were certainly never meant to break a monopoly, and it seemed completely insane to them that anyone might view their small, humble efforts as a threat.

Theresa: When you think about it, it's just so clear.

Jeremy: What is?

Theresa: That we're the ones who believe.

Jeremy: Yes.

Theresa: We're the ones who believe. And they're the ones who deface it.

* * *

Paul had gone out. Silvia was alone in the apartment. They had fought and then, halfway through the disagreement, he simply left. He always ran away from conflict.

Wandering from empty room to empty room, agitated, unable to settle, Silvia thought of packing up everything she owned, throwing every last thing into a few suitcases (she didn't have much), calling a taxi, taking it anywhere – to the airport, getting on the first plane she could find. When he came back she'd be gone. How would he react? How long would it take for him to realize that she wasn't coming back? Days? Weeks? She knew she wouldn't leave, but in her mind it was the most satisfying thought she could possibly imagine.

She wandered into his office. The apartment had five rooms. How come he wrote in his office while she used the kitchen? But she was grasping at straws: This particular instance was not a searing example of patriarchy at work. She actually preferred it this way. She'd feel claustrophobic in an office, with all the books and pictures and history staring down at her. She didn't want a door that could be closed.

On his desk was the manuscript. It was open to the last chapter, the part they had argued about. Had he been rereading it, reconsidering it in light of her recent critique? Probably not, he was far too stubborn for such doubts. She skimmed through the pages: Hitler agreeing to dog-sit when his neighbour goes on vacation, taking the dog for a walk, explaining his theories of racial supremacy as the dog barks in approval, wondering if the dog might be a half-breed or worse, a Jew, buying pet food. On the last page she stopped, her gaze focusing on the last paragraph, as she began to read more closely:

With his pants and underwear around his ankles, Hitler continued to pet and caress the soft black fur of the little mutt. The dog seemed to like this, did not seem to mind his growing - dare he think it - Aryan erection. After a generous application of lube, he entered the dog carefully, worried that its sudden, sharp squeals would alert the neighbours, but already he was too excited to stop, too excited to hold back. After all, he was the Fuehrer, instigator of a thousand-year regime, what did he care what the neighbours thought. Starting with small, soft - he even thought to himself, gentle - thrusts, his gradual petting of the animal increased, and just moments later he was grabbing, grasping onto the fur for traction, holding on for dear life as the dog squirmed and helplessly kicked in every possible direction. "Say fuck me like you mean it," Hitler growled. He was really hammering away now, holding on tight as the dog wheezed and yelped, "Say it! Fucking say it!"

"Fuck me like you mean it," yapped the dog.

5. The Centre for Productive Compromise: An Example of the New Filmmaking

In 1975 Feldmann sent envelopes, each containing a letter and twelve snapshots, to people with whom he was personally acquainted in the local art scene. The amateur-porn style, flash photos showed the artist engaged in a *ménage à trois* with two women in a deep-red brothel-like setting. The letter tells that while he wasn't ashamed to perform such acts in private, their public display was another matter. Yet, he explains, there are much more shameful, "really sickening" things, being done in public, for which the majority feels no shame.

—Roy Arden on Hans-Peter Feldmann

She came up to me in the bar, her shirt half-undone. Maybe not half. Maybe only a few buttons but it was clear where I was looking. She placed her drink on the counter a few inches from my hand. I also held a drink. Our knuckles were almost touching.

"Where's your girlfriend?"

"In the bathroom. Fucking her other guy."

"How many does she have?"

"Right now? Just the two of us. I think. For awhile it might have been up to five."

"Boys and girls?"

"Yeah."

"But now just two?"

"Yeah."

I took a half step towards her. Not even half a step. Really just sliding a couple of inches. Our knuckles were touching, as if we were almost clinking glasses but our hands got in the way.

"If we were to go back to your place, do you think your girl-friend would miss you for a few hours?"

I knew it was best to be honest.

"She might."

"Do you care?"

"If you can live with it, I can."

We were fucking on the edge of the bed when the phone rang, her back on the floor, her legs still on the bed. I didn't quite know how I was balancing, my teeth pressed against her shoulder, one elbow holding almost my full weight. For a moment I thought it was my phone but realized it was hers. Without pulling away she reached over, grabbed her pants from the floor, sliding them towards her, sliding the phone out from the pocket without a thought. She quickly bit my neck then looked back at the phone.

"Keep fucking me, I'm going to take this."

She answered the phone and I did as I was told, listening to only one side of the conversation, doing my best to keep thrust-ing, to guess who it was on the other end of the line. It was dif-ficult to stay focused. I began to drift, lose interest, wondering if Melanie was still in the bathroom, still at the club. I wondered if there'd be a knock on the front door and if it would be her and what might happen then.

Then the phone was up against my ear, her legs wrapping around my hips and she was laughing and thrusting hard up against me. I arched my back.

"It's for you."

The phone was pressed against my ear, everything proceeding naturally.

"Hello," I said into the phone.

"Where did you go?"

"Met someone. Didn't think you'd mind."

"Of course not. You know me. My middle name is 'we have an arrangement.'"

I realized that talking to Melanie changed something: I was thrusting harder now, could hear my voice speaking into the phone, short of breath. I tried to steady myself.

"Why didn't you call on my phone?"

"Thought it would be more fun this way. Anyway, if I'd called your phone you wouldn't have answered."

She had a point. The girl from the bar, still holding the phone to my ear, had managed to flip me over and was on top. I realized I was really enjoying this now, the phone grinding and scratching against my ear as she slammed down into me.

"Call me when you're done?"

"You know I always do."

"Not always, sometimes you fall asleep."

She laughed and I could feel myself getting closer. I wanted to cry out but stifled it.

"You wouldn't by any chance want to join us."

"In your dreams."

As she hung up I started to come.

* * *

The drug we took to remember phone numbers had a side effect. Not quite telepathy, it somehow allowed us to intuit the phone numbers of the people we were with and, if we took a lot, too much, also intuit the numbers of the people *they* were with, as if the telepathy could jump first into our friends and then keep going, jumping into their friends as well. We took it because programming your phone seemed so fucking old-fashioned, so much smoother to actually punch in each digit. But the real reason we took it was the side effect – the ability to phone anyone on any phone. Then things could really begin to slide.

* * *

Steve, on the couch, his pants around his ankles, looking exhausted, drained. Some guy whose name we didn't know perched on top of him, sucking his cock, doing a pretty good job.

Eric was a few feet a way, watching, not watching, he barely knew.

"Eric," Steve said, glancing loosely over at him, "it just drives me into the ground."

"What?"

"My own fucking ambition."

Eric didn't answer but Steve didn't give him a chance.

"Success, new successes . . . I want each one to cure my loneliness. But they don't. Exactly the opposite."

The guy sucking Steve's cock paused for a moment, looked up at Steve and grinned, then went back to work.

Samantha entered, surveyed the room. Steve was taken so she went over to Eric, sat on his lap saddle-style, nuzzling up against his neck. Eric liked Samantha, she was relaxed, ready for anything, took everything else with a grain of salt. And with women he never got hurt. They couldn't quite scratch away at his heart the way men did. He looked over at Steve and slid his hand up the back of Samantha's shirt. Her back was smooth and warm and he felt the first twinge of an erection. They kissed as he felt the familiar disappointment. He whispered in her ear: "Maybe later."

She smiled and laughed lightly. "I know, it's like flipping a coin," she said as she slipped off his lap and went over to fix her hair in the mirror.

It's like flipping a coin was our slang for realizing what you really want. If you flip a coin, it comes up heads, and you suddenly feel that twinge of regret, realizing that what you actually wanted was the tails option – in the end the coin did in fact help you decide. There was a lot of slang like that. Filmmaking meant to really go for it. The Centre for Productive Compromise meant a really good fuck. There were others I can't remember right now.

Eric stood up, walked over to the couch, tapped the blowjob giver on the shoulder. The blowjob giver looked up at him and grinned stupidly. "Do you mind taking a break," Eric said. The guy whose name we didn't know looked over at Samantha who smiled at him. He got up off the couch and walked over to her. Eric looked down at Steve. "Let's find somewhere private," Eric said, "and keep your pants off." Steve pulled himself up off the couch as well, coming to life a little for the first time since the opening three days ago. He stood up, almost stumbling on the pants still wrapped around his ankles but at the same time pulling one leg free, regaining his balance. If he stumbled at all it was only to fall forward into Eric. They wrapped themselves around each other. They kissed.

* * *

The cocktail was the drug to remember phone numbers, the drug to suppress jealousy, the drug to keep you hot and bothered and a little something extra to keep you going all night. The proportions could vary wildly. We all took the cocktail every day, and others who joined us in this practice could quickly enter the stream. The places were The Knife, The Sauna, our various beds and kitchens.

* * *

Maybe Steve had heard about it first or maybe I had. But there was no question: it was the lecture we had been waiting for. We had lined up for tickets, not knowing that not everyone was as enamoured with her as we were, not knowing that it wouldn't even come close to selling out and therefore waiting in line was unnecessary. We didn't care. We took turns making out as we waited. A few others joined in. They didn't take the cocktail (yet) but we didn't mind. If they were willing, we were willing. We had tickets and we went, the auditorium three-quarters full as she took the stage, as we applauded and didn't want to stop. But we stopped because more than anything we wanted to hear her, hear what she had to say, how her thinking had or hadn't changed, how she felt about everything that had come since.

"Many of you might already practice what I like to think of as the new filmmaking," she began, and we glanced at each other along the aisle, smiling half-secretively, as if she knew, as if she were speaking to each one of us personally, or about us as a group. "This, for me, is a practice as rich as it is diverse."

As she was speaking, I wondered if she looked tired, realizing that all the photos I had seen were from a time when she was much younger, that since she began this particular journey she hadn't allowed photographs, so all of them must have been from before.

"For it to become a genre, for it to have any rules whatsoever, is anathema to its very formation. Nonetheless, tonight I will attempt to provide a few basic guidelines. You can take them or leave them. But I have given a great number of talks over the past fifteen years and was beginning to feel that this activity was a bit meaningless if I wasn't willing to take a stand. Because for me the new filmmaking can mean very little if it is not, in some sense, also a new form of humanism, a new form of ethics."

We could not believe what we were hearing. Our hearts sank. Not anarchy, not joy, not freedom, risk and 'the sensational unexpected' – all the reasons we were doing it and loving it and in it for. But humanism, that oldest and emptiest of all shop-worn clichés. I looked down the aisle and could tell we were all thinking the exact same thing. Not only did the emperor have no clothes, but she was artistically bankrupt to a degree that none of us could have previously imagined.

"For me – and of course each of you must find you own entry point and approach – but for me the stories we enact must, on some level, be based on compassion and empathy. Stories of lust, stories of violence, rebellion and betrayal – I do not see how such enactments can add positive meaning to the shared, lived value of the world, the world to which our films both add and simultaneously reimagine."

She had barely even finished this sentence when five audience members stood up and, altogether, with a rather precise efficiency, made for the door. And somehow we knew, even though they were in regular clothes. Without saying a word we stood up and followed. The five of them left and the eight of us followed and every single person in that auditorium was provided an opening, the potential to see the situation, her position, differently, like an electricity striking the room, the perfect little exodus.

The Mascot Front were somehow legends in the new filmmaking community. We had never seen them up close, but we spoke of them often, rumours and hearsay: the two modes at the very heart of our common endeavour. And now we were all standing in the parking lot, looking at each other, angry at our mentor but this anger mitigated by how excited we secretly were to finally meet each other. We knew they had heard of us as well. I'm not sure how we knew, perhaps the same way we intuited phone numbers. And we all stood there in the parking lot, overwhelmed, no one speaking a fucking word. Until finally one of them said, I think he was 'the Popsicle' but there was no way to be sure: "No, it was bound to go this way. I'm not surprised."

We all quietly agreed. We wanted to agree, strengthen this first contact. In retrospect, it did seem inevitable. But if I think back to that ice-pick phrase, a new form of humanism, to the negative ripple it sent through our row as we sat in the auditorium waiting for a light to shine us in the right direction, the only thing I can say for certain is that we had been nothing if not surprised.

* * *

It was a perfectly nondescript suburban house. Every six months this house changed: changed neighbourhoods, changed cities, changed countries, changed forms. This constant changing was one of the many things it meant for them to be underground. From the outside (but were we actually outside?) it seemed exhausting. We went to this house many times over the course of six months. They had just moved there, and after six months they moved again. We did not know exactly where to and, at least so far, were never to visit the new location.

In the basement of that suburban house a man was chained to a radiator. Strangely, he did not seem unhappy about his predicament. We did not know exactly who he was but Steve, also a visual artist, did know who he was and told us he was in fact rather famous, or at least acclaimed within a certain sector of the art world. We no longer knew precisely what we felt about fame – his, our own, or anyone else's.

There was a very beautiful woman who sat a few feet away from the apparently famous man chained to the radiator, a woman whose job it seemed was to sit there and watch over him. She had a box of old sketchbooks in front of her and read and reread them constantly. It seemed to me that the sketchbooks belonged to the man. From time to time the woman would read something to him, or say something, or just look up and stare at him with possibly curious eyes. One time, as she glanced up from a notebook, I overheard her say: "So . . . you really thought we'd make a good art project?" I couldn't precisely identify her tone, she was slippery that way, but I believe a noticeable degree of sarcasm tinted each word. I was in the other room, watching through the doorway, and didn't hear his reply. But I did hear her reply to him. "I don't think I'll ever be able to explain how many unintentional, but also, I don't know . . . pathetic, layers of irony there are in that idea." And she laughed a little, I believe in a rather relaxed way given the situation.

It was also a period during which I was spending much more time alone with Melanie. It was always fantastic with Melanie, and often, when I was with her, I wondered quietly to myself if I even needed the others. It wasn't always fantastic with the others, but sometimes, yes, it was also fantastic, or at least very good. Eric was also spending more time alone with Steve. When we saw them around, they were never together, but when we didn't see them you could pretty much be sure they were entwined. Melanie never stopped by the Mascot house, never came along. Guns made her nervous, that definitely wasn't part of the game she signed on for. Eric also rarely dropped by the house, I believe for similar reasons. Sometimes, when Steve was with me, I had a feeling that Eric was also with Melanie, but couldn't be certain.

And of course, within everything that we were doing and attempting and standing in for, all of that was completely allowed.

* * *

After the talk, Filmmaker A went for a long walk along the river. When she had spoken out against lust and violence, two groups had gotten up and left. She had no idea who they were, but then again she could guess. She was amazed so many people had even come to her talk. She was amazed she could

84

still say something that would incite a dozen or so practitioners to stand up and leave. She knew her star was in decline, could sense it. The new filmmaking was no longer so new. People were no longer startled by it, if they ever had been. But she was trying not to think so much about all that now, though she had been thinking of it a great deal, perhaps too much, over the past few months, wondering what to do, if there was some shift she could make in direction or emphasis that would effectively re-spark things, re-energize at least certain aspects of a waning reception.

Tonight, instead, she found herself thinking of Silvia. She didn't know why she was thinking of Silvia. In fact, she hadn't thought so much about her in many years. A few weeks ago she had heard that soon Silvia would be publishing a book. Perhaps that was what had put the name back in her head. She wondered what the book was about, if there was any chance she might appear in some minor role, in some chapter as a background character. But she didn't actually think it was vague news of an upcoming book that brought Silvia back to mind. It was true what some of them were saying, she was perhaps getting a bit tired, or at least nostalgic. Those first trips overseas, with Silvia at her side: every stop had been so new, fierce and energizing. At the time she would never have thought such things, but now, tonight, walking along the still shimmer of the riverbank, she realized just how much Silvia had contributed to that original excitement and energy.

She wondered if she could call her. She wondered how long it had been since they last spoke. She took out her phone and clicked through the numbers, checking to see if she still had Silvia's in her phone, just to check, just to wonder whether she might have the guts to actually call. She closed her phone and opened it again. As if she couldn't remember whether or not the number was actually there. She closed it again. Stopped. Looked across the river. The night was crisp. She raised her phone and looked at it and as she did so it rang. She was looking at the phone in the foreground, with the river behind it, watching it ring, not recognizing the number. She secretly hoped it was Silvia but knew that that was unlikely if not impossible. She answered.

"Hello."

It was a woman's voice, one she didn't recognize.

"I'm wondering if you'd like to come join me."

She didn't recognize it. She was looking at the river, wondering again, just for a moment, like a split-second flash across her mind, just what the fuck she was doing with her life.

"I'm sorry, who is this?"

"Let's not speak about that for the moment. For now, I have just one question. I'm wondering if I were to give you an address, if you'd like to come join me."

"I'm sorry. I don't understand. Where are you?"

"In my bedroom."

* * *

Samantha lay naked on the bed. Now all she could do was wait. As she waited, she masturbated. She liked the idea of their mentor walking in on her as she was just beginning to stroke herself, a deliciously inappropriate idea, smiling as she thought this, recalling how often they had said to one another that they were free of such restrictions, that they had left the inappropriate behind. She was wet quickly, almost as soon as she reached down, realizing how excited she was by this new scenario, a scenario whipped up on the fly and set into motion with a single phone call, more excited than she previously imagined. She touched herself lightly, charged with the idea of being walked in on, of being walked in on by a woman who had just, albeit indirectly, denounced them to a room of almost three hundred and yet who remained, in some sense, responsible for everything they were doing or had done.

The front door was unlocked. The lights in the downstairs hallway and on the staircase were both on. Her bedroom door was open, the lamp by her bedside also shining. As her excitement grew, she listened for the turn of the door handle, and then she thought she heard it. She imagined the front door now open, her new friend standing in the open doorway, seeing the light, deciding whether or not to go in. The others had complained that their former mentor looked tired, washed up, but to Samantha it was clear exactly how she looked: lonely. She imagined that loneliness drawing Filmmaker A down the hallway, up the stairs, and as she imagined, she heard footsteps, rubbing herself more firmly now, feeling her breathing become just that little bit more quick, more sharp, imagining how these sharp, sweet breaths might sound in the staircase, in the downstairs hall – enticing – and turning her head towards the door, stroked the inside of her thigh with her other hand.

As she started to come she realized that Filmmaker A was already sitting at the foot of the bed, looking uncomfortable, not looking at her at all. Samantha must have closed her eyes for a moment, not noticed her come in. She stopped moving her fingers but didn't remove her hand.

"Why don't you take off your clothes?"

Filmmaker A didn't look over but started to silently undress. Samantha slowly sat up, slid towards her, and began to help, kissing her neck, her shoulders, her back, unclasping her bra, slowly caressing her inner thighs.

"Aren't you glad you came?" Samantha purred, her lips just a few inches from their mentor's, licking and gently biting.

Filmmaker A stopped, went limp. She had started to caress Samantha but now stopped.

"I don't know. There's something I don't like."

"But there's so much to like." Samantha kissed her again, stroked her face and kissed her neck, all to no response.

"I don't like the fact this isn't real."

* * *

During the few months we were allowed to hang out at the Mascot house, the famous artist chained to the radiator exerted a strange fascination upon us. In the art press he had been reported missing, presumed dead. Museums were considering the possibility of posthumous retrospectives. His prices were skyrocketing.

There in the basement, the beautiful woman sitting just a few feet away from him, patiently flipping through a seemingly endless series of notebooks, he seemed amused, sometimes tired but just as often alert and engaged. The woman flipping through the notebooks was genuinely striking, it seemed obviously he was in love. We often asked the other Mascots about him, about both of them, but as usual were given little information.

It occurred to me that while, for both us and the Mascots, our activities were strong examples of the new filmmaking, for him, being chained to that radiator, watched over by a woman he was growing to love, was in a similar way an artwork, perhaps an artwork he was hoping would last for the rest of his life.

The first time I spoke to him – a short conversation as I stood in the doorway and, for obvious reasons, he remained in place – I was startled to realize he knew nothing about the new filmmaking. That, from his perspective, the activities of the Mascots were considerably more real. And also that the Mascots continued to conceal this crucial piece of information, as if no one wanted to let him in on a joke.

I thought of how many of us were drinking the cocktail now, how there must be people taking the cocktail, perhaps many, who also didn't know. And I found myself appreciating the delicate pleasure of these subtle slippages between filmmaking and pure reality, how when filmmaking was at its best the two were so evocatively indistinguishable.

Also during this first conversation he told me how, before he came here, he had been working on a piece or series about the Mascot Front. And how, over the course of working on this particular theme, the project had sent him into a kind of crisis, led him towards the conclusion that making work for galleries was rather feeble when compared to the much more dangerous pursuit of attempting real interventions within politics or society. How of course there had been various times in history during which artists had been persecuted, but in his lifetime they had not, and persecution itself felt like evidence of a richness and validity he had come to see as artistic, alluding to the fact that no one we knew had been more persecuted than the Mascots.

I agreed with him hesitantly, feeling uncomfortable that I possessed certain information he did not, at the same time not

wanting to upset the overall balance of the situation by revealing anything the Mascots did not wish to be revealed. Just then
the woman returned – it was strange I never learned her name –
and her arrival signalled the end of our short conversation. She
picked a notebook off the top of the pile and continued to read.

* * *

Steve and Eric sat in Steve's studio, every kind of possible object
and configuration of objects strewn around them. Eric was
naked, Steve fully dressed, Steve's hand tightly gripping Eric's
erection, both crying, but crying in a manner that brought
them closer together. Still crying, Steve brought his face down
towards Eric's cock and rubbed his tears against the foreskin,
wetting it, licking off the tears with short, sad but playful licks.
They didn't know exactly why they were crying. Maybe they
were only crying in order to try something new together, they
had already done so much, or maybe it just happened naturally,
the way tears sometimes do.

They had started crying in discussion, a discussion that
began when Eric said he wanted to talk about the films, wondering, the way one wonders aloud to a lover, if they were still
fun, still vital. Noticing that sometimes he felt bored or jealous, and yet within the scripts neither boredom nor jealousy
were allowed, and how dirty never felt quite dirty enough if you
couldn't honestly speak your mind. And they had started to talk
about jealousy, Steve saying that so often in the very best scenes
jealousy was the subtext, the unspoken element that made
everything, every element and moment, more compelling,
conflicted, alive. As Steve took Eric more fully in his mouth, the

tears slowing but not stopping completely, Eric reached over, as slowly as possible undoing Steve's fly, then just as teasingly starting on the belt buckle. As he did so he remembered how, just minutes ago, he had been so insistent that he didn't want jealousy to *always* be the subtext (did it have to be so repetitive?). Sometimes he wanted the subtext to be love.

* * *

I told Melanie about the man chained to the radiator and the woman watching over him. She seemed intrigued, more interested than I had expected. Before she had refused to join me on my many excursions to the Mascot house but now, suddenly, she wanted to. I thought maybe she wanted to fuck the beautiful woman or the man chained to the radiator or both. I thought maybe I wanted to watch or join in. I imagined various scenarios, scripting them in my head as we stood at the front door and I gave the correct password.

In the front room several versions of each Mascot outfit hung, newly pressed and cleaned, ready replacements for the ones being worn somewhere out in the world at this very moment. I was watching Melanie carefully, trying to sense her reaction to each room, each new thing. The outfits seemed to attract her, as she took a few steps towards them, looking back at me with a smile.

It had taken me weeks to figure out who went with which outfit. Bear was the tall solid one, in some sense I thought of her as the leader, though I also knew very well that, from their perspective, they had no ongoing leaders. (She was in the room with us now.) Rabbit was short, maybe South Asian or Portuguese, I was never a particularly good judge of such things. Tortoise looked kind of tough, barely spoke. I believed he was the one who organized most of the weapons. Melanie turned away from the outfits and smiled at Bear, who smiled back. "You've killed people?" she asked.

"What kind of question is that?" Bear wasn't offended, still smiling slyly.

"Just trying to get a feel for the territory."

"There are between 150 million and 1.5 billion insects for every human being on earth. We've both killed insects but they're by far the majority. What does it mean to keep things in proportion?"

"That's a completely fucked analogy." I could tell Melanie was enjoying this now. That she was glad she had come. "We don't say human life is sacred because we're the majority. It's sacred because we're human too."

"We'll kill an insect because it stabs us with the tiniest sting, over a single drop of blood. The people I've killed were coming at me with much larger weapons."

"But why were they coming at you? You have to take some responsibility. It's not without reason."

"We're just trying to live another way." Bear became pensive, looking straight at Melanie, then down at the ground. "It should be allowed."

Melanie turned back to look at the outfits again. "Is it all right if I touch them?"

And because she was Melanie she didn't wait for an answer, slowly walking along the row, running her hand across the fur, looking over at me in complicity, slowing down as she neared the end of the row, ready for more.

* * *

The phone rang and Steve answered it. "You'll never guess who I'm fucking right now."

"Who?"

"Come see for yourself."

Steve and Eric arrived quickly. Samantha got up from bed, completely naked and soaked in sweat, hugging them both, kissing them on the lips, giving it a little bit of tongue.

Filmmaker A felt embarrassed to be caught naked, worse by two men, and covered herself with the sheet. She thought maybe she had fallen asleep for a moment, or maybe she had only been hovering between consciousness and dream. Either way she felt interrupted, this new influx of people, people from a group she had in some sense created. She knew little about them, only through rumour, and therefore wasn't sure if anything she knew was correct. They all piled onto the bed, introducing themselves, covering her, she almost thought consuming her. She didn't like this, tried to pull herself free.

"Maybe we could go get something to eat."

In the restaurant they kept asking questions. It was as if they wanted to know everything, what she thought, how she lived, when, where and why she worked. But as the questions kept coming she realized in fact they only wanted to know one thing, they wanted to know what she thought of them.

"No one thinks they're going to have an impact when they start something," she tried to explain, "or maybe you think you're going to have an impact, but at the same time you think it's only hubris, chances are slim, better to focus on your own thing and let everything else take care of itself."

"But now you have had an impact," Eric interrupted. "What do you think of it all now."

"I don't know." She didn't know. And the parts she did know she didn't want to share. "It's overwhelming."

"We thought the new filmmaking was about blurring the line between what's scripted and real. And there's nothing more real than sex."

"Death is more real." It just slipped out. It was absolutely the last thing she meant or wanted to say. She was nervous, uncomfortable, it was unlike her. "I'm sorry, I didn't mean that anyone should die." It was unlike her to apologize.

"But that's what's so powerful about the new filmmaking," Steve was really trying to persuade her. "When you fuck you really fuck, when you die you really die."

"I suppose." She was being evasive. She didn't like this line of reasoning. This wasn't what she had meant. She had only been searching for ways to make her life more vibrant, more alive, and to make this very vibrancy her art. Fucking and dying didn't feel alive, at least not in the way she had meant.

"You don't seem convinced."

"I don't know." There was always some way out. "When you're an artist, if you're a real artist, in some sense you always have to kill the father. That's our legacy: the modernist break."

"So you do want someone to die," Steve joked.

"I don't know. You wouldn't think I'd want it to be me."

They absolutely insisted she come home with them but she refused, refused again and was becoming a drag so eventually they gave up and let her be. She sat alone in the restaurant. They had left without paying so, unthinkingly, she took care of the bill. They had explained to her the cocktail, the cell phones, the Centre for Productive Compromise. She had to admit, it did sound like a good film but she didn't want to live it. It didn't matter if they were right and she was wrong and of course there was no right or wrong. She didn't know what to think, how to defend her position or even what her position was any more. They had done this to her, opened something up, not much but a little, and she found herself, almost against her will, begrudgingly admiring them for it. Something had opened. In all of this there must be something she could use.

* * *

As predicted, Melanie walked straight up to the man chained to the radiator and started making out.

The beautiful woman looked up from her notebook, sitting just a few feet away, and watched, as from the doorway I watched all three. It was an unspoken rule in the Centre for Productive Compromise that men were allowed to be sexually aggressive towards men, and woman were allowed to be sexually aggressive towards men, but men were not allowed to be sexually aggressive towards women. This was one of the many ways we tried to keep things safe. Of course anyone could say no at any time, though most of us rarely chose this option, but a 'no' had to be immediately respected.

The famous artist chained to the radiator pulled half an inch away from Melanie and said no.

"Are you sure?" Melanie asked.

He was sure.

Melanie walked across the room and sat in a chair in the corner. She looked over at the woman still holding the notebook.

"Maybe you'd like to watch me and her go at it instead?"

The man chained to the radiator looked at the beautiful woman and then back at Melanie. For a moment it seemed he was considering it. He was still looking at Melanie. "What kind of Mascot are you?"

"What do you mean?"

He gestured towards the beautiful woman. "She's a tortoise? What are you?"

Melanie thought for a split second before clicking in. "I'm not a Mascot."

"I thought everyone here was a Mascot."

"You're only hot for Mascots?"

The man considered this for a moment. It was as if the things he had found, up until this point, most profound and provocative, had suddenly been sexualized, as if he was considering whether this new (at least to him) more sexual interpretation was accurate.

"I wanted to come here." He finally said. "Before they kidnapped me, I had wanted to come here, to meet them, to somehow be a part of all this." I didn't know he had been kidnapped, though the moment he said it of course it made perfect sense. "Before I came here, I was struggling, grasping at straws, struggling to maintain a position that was no longer tenable. Being here has simplified things. I am chained down. I am brought food. I am unchained in order to wash and exercise. And it has also simplified my thoughts. I ask myself what is important, and the answer is simple: What the Mascots are fighting for is important. The way they want to live, playful and strange, at odds with everything else we think we know. They are not consumers, they are reinventing cosmopolitanism, reinventing what it means to believe in something and fight. The longer

I stay here, the more I admire them. So yes, if that's what you mean by being hot only for Mascots, I suppose it's true."

Melanie looked bored. She was never one for lofty speeches. She liked fire and she liked action. But I was fascinated. With no knowledge of the new filmmaking, that artist chained to the radiator was in the moment, everything he experienced more precarious, more vital. His struggle never paused, while our knowledge of each activity as being 'only' new filmmaking somehow dampened our understanding of it. With the Centre for Productive Compromise I had always felt, if we got bored, we could stop at any moment, but if the Mascots stopped they would be rounded up and killed. I felt enormous admiration for them, seeing them anew through his eyes.

"I guess that's a no," Melanie replied. "You don't want to watch her and I go at it?"

The man laughed. "Before I came here there would have been nothing I'd have liked more."

* * *

Eric and Samantha were excited, buzzing from the 'mentor encounter,' but Steve was morose. He was questioning, silently, for himself, everything they had been doing and why. Their mentor had somehow thrown him off, the way she seemed so faded, and the more he thought about it, the more it seemed to him that in all of this there was some great, stark irony. She had started the new filmmaking in order to live more fully, more vitally, and yet after twenty years of practice she now seemed like someone with little investment in life. Steve wondered if a similar fate awaited the Centre for Productive Compromise, if all their cinematic adventures were somehow a road that led in only one direction: toward exhaustion and disillusionment. When they had tried everything, what would be left to try?

He wanted to share these thoughts with Samantha and Eric, but the meeting apparently had the opposite effect on them. Samantha seemed particularly emboldened by her recent conquest, excited and energized by new possibilities. She began giddily proposing new scenarios.

"So let's say Silvia, we all remember Silvia . . ."

Eric nodded that they did.

"Silvia's at The Knife, she stops by there from time to time, doesn't she, and her phone rings and it's me. I'm phoning her from bed. I'm in bed with the mentor, post-coital, holding hands or being spooned. The mentor doesn't know who I'm calling, but she's used to me calling strange people at strange times so thinks nothing of it, and Silvia doesn't know who I'm with. And Steve comes up to Silvia at The Knife . . ."

Steve had been distracted, hadn't been listening closely, but at the mention of his name clicked back in.

"Steve approaches Silvia at the bar, introduces himself, says he's a friend of Paul. All this time Silvia is still on the phone with me . . ."

It was unnerving how much Samantha knew about Silvia, Paul, their mentor and the rest of the circle. Like how some people might collect baseball cards or celebrity gossip, she tried to follow, through rumour, hearsay and the odd notice in the press, whatever she could about their mentor's life.

"So Steve is with Silvia and I'm with the mentor. Then, next, I'm not sure. There's just so many ways it could go . . ."

"Does Silvia hang up on you when Steve arrives or does she stay on the line?"

"Stays on the line, of course."

"What are you two talking about?"

Samantha thought for a moment before letting the scenario unfold: "I'm telling her that the sex in her last book is some of the best sex I've ever read. That there are so many things I'd love to act out, so many things we could try together. She jokes that I better be on the left, because if I'm on the right it might prove fatal. The mentor doesn't know who I'm talking too, but hears me mention a book and becomes suspicious. She's cagey around talk of Silvia's book. We're talking about whether her book could be a kind of script or scenario for new filmmaking. Whether or not there's ever been a new filmmaking literary adaptation, and how this idea might be one possible way forward. The mentor is listening, her curiosity peaked by all this talk of new filmmaking, and of course at the bar Steve is also listening."

"This is like a porn movie with no porn," Steve interrupted.

"I thought you loved scenarios with a long, slow build," Samantha teased. "The anticipation . . ."

"I love scenarios where everyone's in on the game. Where everyone's cocktail-ready and primed."

"You don't know that I can't convince Silvia and our mentor to join the cocktail."

"I don't want to convince anyone, makes it too much like a cult. For me, I've always preferred when people spontaneously join the fun."

"You're so uptight sometimes . . ." She was about to lay into him but stopped herself. So much was going on here. In fact, Steve was always a bit cagey when talking about their mentor. Perhaps there was some jealousy. In many ways he was already their leader-by-default. Perhaps, on some level, it pissed him off that no matter what he did, how clever or sharp he was, there would always be someone over his head. In some ways their mentor was like original sin, proof that no matter what they did the Centre for Productive Compromise would never be entirely their own.

Samantha could see why all of this might bother Steve, with his razor-sharp ambition and desire to see through everything to the core, but really she couldn't care less. For her, Filmmaker A was inspiring: no more, no less. There was no substitute for the kinds of liberation she had found through seeing certain situations in her life as scenarios, in scripting them and by scripting them, taking control. And there was no question that Filmmaker A had single-handedly made this liberation, such swift and joyous rushes of freedom, possible.

* * *

Melanie was fascinated. Maybe it was only that she wasn't used to being turned down, but I don't think so. For me, her fascination had about it something strange and convincing. Now, each time I visited the house she would accompany me, grilling each of the Mascots in turn, trying to understand what made them tick, how their version of filmmaking could be so different from ours and, at the same time, so complementary. Feeling out opportunities for seduction, for new and striking scenarios we could all soon play out together, yet finding none. It was curious that they put up with her questions, graciously, as if it was the most normal thing in the world. Perhaps in some sense they liked the attention.

Melanie was talking to the Kangaroo as I, once again, watched from across the room.

K: It's true we're not born this way. Yes, it's a decision. We decide to wear the outfits, but once you've made the decision it's a commitment, it's like your skin colour has changed. No one who becomes a Mascot ever decides to turn back.

M: It's the same for us. When we sign on, we sign on for life. But . . . I mean, there are moments when I'm lying awake at night, when I have doubts, when I wonder just what the fuck I'm doing with my life.

K: We don't doubt, we fight. There's no time. As soon as you pause for reflection you're dead.

From across the room the dynamic was clear. Melanie was playful, flirting, curious, feeling out the situation, the boundaries of its honesty, tasting it for pleasure. But Kangaroo was focused, looking straight ahead, fielding each question like a knife.

K: When Popsicle was killed . . .

M: How did he die?

K: Two bullets in the back of the head as he was getting into the shower. It was the first time someone was assassinated – there've been a few since – but it was the first time one of us was killed out of outfit, couldn't defend ourselves, didn't get caught in the line of fire. We had a big meeting with everyone. Popsicle was our favourite. Everyone fucking loved that guy. There was no one better. And we asked the question straight. This shit is more dangerous than we ever imagined. If anyone here wants to leave, go for it. Everyone here will understand, no one will judge you. And no one flinched, no one budged. To be honest I don't know why. Maybe it was only out of respect for Popsicle.

M: The thing is I don't believe you. Everyone has doubts. It's only human.

K: Maybe when you put on the outfit you're not exactly a person anymore. In some sense you become animal. And your instincts keep telling you that the fight is just.

* * *

Filmmaker A was scheduled to speak the next day in Spain but she cancelled her flight. Did she want to fuck Samantha again, she wondered to herself. Was her curiosity about these oversexed acolytes only a pretext to get some more action? Or was there, as she suspected or at least hoped, more to it? Did she see in these Productive Compromisers some glimpse of her former self, her former idealism? And in such a glimpse might she hope to reignite her practice?

And then she had the perverse idea that would change everything: She would go out and buy at 16 mm camera. She would use the old filmmaking, which was of course where she began, to make a documentary about the new filmmaking. Could she actually do this? Was it a stroke of genius or a betrayal of everything she had stood for and believed in over the past twenty years? She didn't know, but it was an idea, a new direction, and she was hungry enough for new directions that she had to give it a try.

* * *

Steve was examining his eye in the mirror when Eric got home. There was definitely some bruising and it fucking hurt. Eric glanced through the bathroom door, catching sight of the mirror, and headed into the kitchen for ice. He had been bashed in the park about two years ago and had basically avoided the park since. He walked into the bathroom, pulled a towel off the rack and poured in the contents of the ice tray, holding the frozen towel against Steve's eye.

"Was it an ambush or a show?"

"A show."

"What was the script?"

"I was going to tell him I didn't love him, I loved you. We'd kiss then he'd punch me in the face. Then we'd fuck. You were supposed to be here to watch, maybe join in, but he was early."

Eric laughed and as he laughed he realized that he almost wanted to cry. It was like a new filmmaking love letter. He wished he had been here to see it.

"He only punched me once. But he was stronger than he looked."

And then they were both laughing, the ice scattering onto the floor as they kissed.

Later that night they were planning a visit to the Mascot house. Everyone was invited yet no one knew why. Eric joked that Steve's black eye would lend them cred, show that their brand could be just as tough as the Mascots, but the joke fell flat since they both knew they were nowhere near as tough as the Mascots. The discrepancy defied humour.

* * *

Samantha opened the door and her mentor was already film-ing. That first shot, the close-up of Samantha with the 16 mm right up in her face, her expression a mix of absolute surprise and potential betrayal, that first shot was enough to suggest to Filmmaker A that she had struck a vein.

Later, as she watched the footage in the editing suite, she was startled by the nuance and complexity of Samantha's reactions. As she replayed it over and over again, thinking of where to cut, wondering if the most interesting thing might be to simply leave the reel intact, dead moments and all, she found herself making a list of the contradictory aspects of Samantha's 'performance':

1) She likes being watched.

2) Being watched by a technical apparatus is a new experi-ence for her.

3) This new experience is titillating but also suspicious.

4) Flirting with the camera. Flirting with me through the camera.

5) She has an ideological love of the new filmmaking. She is not sure if this love also means she must have an ideo-logical hatred of the old filmmaking.

6) How to reconcile her ideology with this newfound excitement of being filmed.

7) Moments of self-questioning. Had her ideology been arrived at through a reasonable process or had she rushed into it, arrived at it rashly.

8) Questioning her mentor. If her mentor was regressing towards the old filmmaking, then perhaps her mentor was bogus all along.

9) Or, on the contrary, if her mentor is endorsing the old filmmaking perhaps it is the wave of the future.

10) Is flirting with the camera valid? Should I restrain myself? Or modulate my performance in some way.

11) I think I am falling in love with her.

Was Samantha falling in love as well? Or was it only Filmmaker A falling in love with Samantha? She watched the footage again. She had forgotten the pleasure of watching the same take over and over, catching different aspects and shadings every time as the celluloid rolled through the flatbed.

Samantha walking from the front door towards the kitchen, glancing back over her shoulder, smiling, offering coffee or a drink, as the camera follows a few feet behind, trying to keep the shot steady, keep Samantha centred in the frame, her own voice patiently off-camera:

"How long have you been doing the Centre for Productive Compromise?"

"I don't know. A couple of years. That's not a very interesting question. I thought you were creative."

"What would be a more interesting question?"

"I don't know. Do you want to fuck?"

"All right. Do you want to fuck?"

"Not on camera. That's boring."

Samantha making espresso, at the same time pouring them both a shot of something strong, from the angle possibly tequila or rum, and the camera pans down and over as the coffee and shot glass are placed on the table beside her, and she remembered how she wondered if she should drink or instead concentrate on filming.

"For you excitement is important? Excitement is an important part of new filmmaking?"

"You say that like excitement is a bad thing."

"No, I don't think that."

"Isn't that why you're here, in my house? Looking for excitement?"

Samantha knocking back the shot and her last sip of coffee. She heads down the hall, up the stairs, towards the bedroom as the camera follows.

"Maybe you could give us an example of how the new filmmaking works."

"You'd like an example? All right. I was lying here in bed. We had all just walked out of your lecture and I was thinking of you. I had an idea, concocted a scenario. I would phone you, give my address but not my name, lie here in bed, undress, leave the front door unlocked, see if you would come."

As she speaks Samantha stretches out on the bed. She takes the perfect pause before continuing:

"You know the rest."

* * *

I had never seen so many people crammed into the house. In fact, there was barely room for all of us. Video monitors and cameras had been set up in every corner. You could participate in the meeting from any room. I recognized the Mascots and Productive Compromisers, I think basically all of us were there, but there were so many others I had never seen before. Every kind of person: businessmen, street punks, religious sects, people from other parts of the world in traditional dress. (I felt ignorant, not knowing precisely what parts of the world they were from.) So many characters, kinds of characters, I was unable to place or identify. It seemed the Mascots really got around. They had managed to draw together an entire spectrum of the unexpected.

Melanie and I pushed through the crowd, gradually shoving our way from room to room with no particular purpose. No one seemed to know when the meeting would start or what it was about. There was much curiosity and speculation. Steve was in a corner watching the action with a strange expression, far removed from his usual anxious bemusement.

"Who the fuck are all these people?"

I shrugged and smiled.

"They're the international, worldwide Mascot super-fan club," Melanie said, scanning the room for potential conquests. I took a moment to admire how even at the heart of a political meeting she could continue to cruise.

"Maybe our gang should get out there a bit more, go forth in the world, get organized." Steve continued scanning the room, trying to make sense of it all. "It's like we're the local burger joint and they're fucking McDonald's."

It's true I also felt this strange kind of jealousy. They say sex sells, but it now seemed that the unlikely combination of guns plus furry outfits was selling much better. In every room there was such a palpable sense of excitement. I felt that, like us, most of the people here had assumed they were the only ones who knew about the Mascots, who were in on the secret, everyone just as surprised as us to learn there were so many supporters. We spotted Samantha on the far side of the room. She didn't see us and was gone before we made it over.

The epicentre of the meeting appeared to be the basement, surrounding the famous artist still chained to the radiator. On all monitors one could see a large group of Mascots, most in outfit but a handful not, sitting in a semicircle whose open side faced the radiator. Microphones were being set up. Nothing seemed forced, but everything contributed to a perpetual build in anticipation. From what we knew and could see, the Mascots never had a leader, power seemed to continuously shift among them, within smaller or larger groups that operated autonomously. There may well have been some functional structure behind it, but if so it remained invisible. Then, very suddenly, a loud bell rang ten times. A microphone was handed to the famous artist. His voice sounded clearly through every room.

"I have been asked to chair this meeting. I suppose I was asked because I'm thought to be a bit neutral, not exactly a Mascot, something of an outsider. However, as many of you already know, I do not consider myself neutral in any way. From my perspective, I am a complete and total partisan of the Mascot Front and their ongoing battle. But perhaps that is beside the point.

"The Mascot Front have called this meeting because, for the first time, they now wish for others to fight alongside them. The only way against failure, and towards success, is solidarity. In the past, the Mascot Front has attempted to do no damage to anyone other than those who were directly attacking them, like the Hippocratic oath: first rule, do no harm. But now the situation has become considerably more dire, and if anyone here chooses to fight alongside us in the future, it is possible, even likely, that you might be injured or killed. This is the shift, the possible change in our policy, that we have come together to question and discuss."

It was then I noticed her. In the bottom corner of the screen our mentor was perched, a 16 mm camera on her shoulder, filming everything that occurred. Shock is not quite the right word for what ran through me at that moment. It was like I had taken the world's strongest drug. Everything I knew, or thought I knew, was turned inside out. If I had seen her holding a live octopus it would have made more sense, at that moment, than to see her filming. Later, when we were all speaking about it at The Knife, many mentioned a sense of betrayal, that they felt betrayed by her return to the old filmmaking, but I'm not sure what I felt was betrayal, it was more like a sense of unreality, that I couldn't quite grasp the logic or trajectory of what was unfolding before me. I wondered if this was in part because I was watching it on a monitor, in somewhat imperfect focus, like a video in a gallery, yet at the same time knew it was happening just underneath my feet. I pointed it out to Melanie – pointing to the exact corner of the screen – and for a moment I thought she would scream. But then she fell silent, said nothing.

"In one sense it is true, what we are looking for here tonight are volunteers, volunteers to fight by our side, volunteers to help us survive. But in another sense we are searching for something more. We feel ready to open up, to question the basic assumptions of our strategy, which we now must admit is failing us. We are here to ask all of you to think about the question together: how can we still win."

There was a pause as a microphone was handed to Bear.

"A meeting like this is a strange beast." Bear continued, "All of you know something about the Mascot Front but few of you know very much. This has perhaps, up till now, been our fatal flaw. The fact that almost no one knows just how bad things have gotten, that we now believe we are practically on the verge of extinction, also prevents anyone from offering assistance. Of the four hundred Mascots we are aware of, we now believe over two hundred have been killed or are currently imprisoned. Another ninety Mascots are missing in action. Many of the missing have most likely done little more than hang up their outfits – a grave error, in our judgment, but nonetheless the best-case scenario. However, we cannot rule out the possibility that of these ninety missing some have been killed as well. To the best of our knowledge, between eighty and one hundred Mascots are here with us tonight and the most likely scenario is that, within one year from now, half of us will be captured or dead and in three years time, there will be no one. Those who know me will also know I have fought fearlessly for my entire adult life. But right now, I must admit, I'm afraid."

Another silence. I was listening, thinking about everything I had heard, all viewed through the lens of our mentor's sudden reversal. And as I listened one thing became increasingly clear. A gradual reversal of my own. A moment of clarity. What I realized was that all of this, our encounter and complicity with the Mascots, had been a misunderstanding. They weren't new filmmakers at all, they were actual revolutionaries, fighting for their rights, subject to real and constant persecution. We had viewed the entirety of their activities through our own strange screen, assuming they were like us, not seeing or admitting the key, radical difference.

Melanie saw Samantha, again on the far side of the room, grabbed my hand and pulled us towards her. The crowd was denser now, all standing, staring at the various monitors, wondering, as I was, how much they cared. Would we, any of us, risk our lives to fight alongside these relative strangers? How many of us were even considering it? Was I? (Of course I was considering it but was I really giving the matter serious thought?)

When we reached Samantha, Melanie wasted no time: "Our mentor has a new friend."

"You have no idea."

Samantha told us about her session, how she was filmed, then they had sex, and how this was the first sex she'd had in years that she was unable to think of as filmmaking.

"It was so strange: we were fucking, and I realized there wasn't this other layer intertwined with it. Suddenly we were just fucking. There were no scenarios, no shots, no set-ups. When she put down the camera all of that was put aside as well."

"She regained control."

"How do you mean?"

"Before it was your film. You called her. You were writing the scenario. Now, with the camera on her shoulder, it's hers again. She topped you."

Samantha look distressed, more distressed than I ever recalled seeing her. She obviously hadn't thought of it this way. A moment ago she was feeling liberated, emboldened by this new experience of fucking without a scenario, and now she felt she'd been played, that she'd lost the upper hand. It's amazing how fast these switches can flip.

On the monitor Kangaroo, in full outfit, was continuing: "And I think what's most important in this dialogue is to remember that we are never only victims. Yes we were persecuted. But we were persecuted and we fought back, knowing, as we did so, that we were beginning a cycle of vengeance we might not be able to stop. For now, the danger is clear: If we don't change something, if we don't alter our strategy, this vengeance will consume us completely. It has only been in the past few months that we have begun to consider the idea of a truce. It is now, in our minds at least, on the table. But it is difficult to negotiate a truce from a position of such desperate weakness. That is why we are asking for your help. In the immediacy of the present we must strengthen our hand."

I was fixated on the monitor, while still listening to Melanie and Samantha with one ear. That is how I learned that our mentor, who I could catch only a glimpse of in the bottom corner of the screen, was making a documentary on the new filmmaking, focusing, at least to start, on us and the Mascots, and I realized that she had made the exact same mistake as us, had not yet realized what was really at stake.

The meeting was being opened up to the floor and a man in the next room was speaking into a microphone: "Unlike many people here, I've had more than a few experiences with armed resistance."

He was thin, focused, spoke as if he meant it.

"And I admire the pure insanity of the Mascot Front, as I would admire any noble yet lost cause."

On the monitor the Mascots were listening intensely, tilting their heads towards the speakers on the floor.

"The difficulty, as I see it, is so obvious as to be almost not worth mentioning. When you are in uniform you are too conspicuous. You are like big, furry, moving targets. And when you are out of uniform you have disavowed the very thing you are fighting for. However, I believe you are already well on your way to a solution: A secondary, non-Mascot rebel force could do the jobs Mascots are simply too conspicuous for. And, in additional support of this idea, I would simply like to state one more thing. In my experience, to fight for a cause, to risk one's life in support of a cause one truly believes in, is the only way to give one's life actual content and meaning. Everything else is just for show."

It was difficult to gauge how the others around us were responding to such bold statements of intent. The air in the room was tense and ambiguous. The Mascots too were taking a moment to quietly confer before responding. And it was within this relative silence, this murmur of perplexed consideration, that I first heard the clatter in the front room. It was strange, those early moments when I still thought nothing of it. I wondered about the new filmmaking, what the implications were if the Mascots in fact had absolutely nothing to do with it, what it meant for us, for our practice, for our debauched scenarios, the commotion in the front room getting louder and I thought, for a split second, I heard a muffled gunshot without quite registering it, nothing was clear, it could have been anything. The Mascots on the small screen began to scatter, to energize, reaching for things off-screen, most likely weapons.

In one sense everyone around us was attempting to push, to run, but the rooms were so crowded, we were so tightly packed together, that no one could get very far or move very fast. We were being pushed from all sides, but I still hadn't seen anything. I asked Melanie which way she thought we should go and she said we should stay put, cling to the wall, keep our eyes open and, if things got worse, drop to the floor. I pressed against the wall, pressed up beside her. Through the doorway I caught a glimpse of full riot gear and on the television screen twelve empty chairs formed a semicircle beside the famous artist still chained to the radiator. He looked straight ahead, a bit frightened, and then, almost to still his own fears, stretched his entire body across the floor and managed to reach one of the microphone cords, dragging the microphone towards him. There was more gunfire, a series of louder bursts much closer to us as the famous artist began to speak.

"I don't know exactly what's happening. There seems to be some degree of panic. I assume this is something like a raid . . ."

People were running in front of him, running between him and the video camera. It wasn't clear how to get out but everyone tried.

"However, in such situations, whatever the situation might be, it's always best to remain calm. There are four exits on the ground floor plus two fire escapes upstairs. Please find your way to the one you think nearest . . ."

Kangaroo ran into the frame with a machine gun in one hand and a crowbar in the other, slid the crowbar between the radiator and the handcuffs, effortlessly snapping them open. The famous artist stood up, dropped the microphone, which hit the floor loudly, and was out of frame in a split second as a few feet away from us a man fell face forward, blood trickling out from under him. I suddenly wondered why I wasn't more afraid.

I whispered to Melanie that we should head for the front door, the violence seemed to be moving towards the back, maybe the front was clearing, and as I was doing so our mentor slid into the room, camera on her shoulder, a huge smile on her face as she scanned the room for a moment worth filming. She was also heading towards the front so it now seemed we were following her, the camera making her task more difficult as she crammed through the melee, clearing a path for us, now less conspicuous in her shadow.

Police were pushing through every room. I thought I counted thirty, but there must have been more, from the noise it felt like there were even more outside, the occasional bullet crack over a constant soundtrack of banging and pushing. I assumed they were looking for Mascots but it was hard to tell, difficult to understand anything. They were shooting out surveillance cameras, smashing television screens, throwing people towards the walls, onto the floor, out of the way, though there was nowhere to go. Our mentor was less than a foot in front of us, 16 mm still rolling, when an officer spotted her, grabbing her camera roughly as she continued to cling to it, and they were both thrown towards the wall because she would not let go – then a kind of awkward clatter between her, the camera and the officer, until without warning another officer's rifle smashed hard against her face, splitting open her nose, blood streaming down over her clothes, in seconds forming a river on the ground, the camera in pieces against the floor, another officer already ripping, clawing out the film, as our mentor crumpled down and we rushed forward to catch her.

6. The Frightening Thing Is Everyone Has Their Reasons

There are no norms. All people are exceptions to a rule that doesn't exist.

—Fernando Pessoa

I went to get my hair cut in Berlin. The moment I sat down in the chair I could already sense that the hairdresser didn't much like me. "Fucking American tourists," I could almost hear him thinking to himself as he brought the scissors closer to my head. "Trendy capitalist shit pigs."

And he had barely begun to cut my hair but already I could feel it was going to be one of the worst haircuts I'd had in a long time. And I wondered if he was doing it on purpose while at the same time imagining someone else: another German hairdresser, vaguely aware of the Dadaists and having experienced expressionism and the neo-pathetic cabaret just before he left for New York in the forties or fifties, who more than anything hated the fucking stupid Americans that came to get their hair cut from him day in and day out.

And since he was convinced the Americans were completely stupid, he began to experiment, see what he could get away with, cutting away big clumpy bald patches into the sides of people's heads and, when they complained, telling them that it was the new style back in Germany. Most never came back and yet he started getting a new kind of client: young artists and bohemians in search of styles that ran contrary to the conservative, bourgeois values of the previous generation.

The title of this chapter is stolen from a line of dialogue – or more precisely from a subtitle (since I do not speak or understand French) – that is to be found in the classic Renoir film *La Règle du jeu*. The film, which I've seen only once (something like twenty years ago) made barely the slightest of impressions upon me (even at the time) and yet this single line of dialogue nonetheless continues to strike me anew, incessantly and in the most singularly piercing fashion. Somehow it summarizes everything. The frightening thing is that everyone has their reasons, and somehow whatever anyone does, whatever anyone does to you or for you, they are more often than not able to justify it to themselves in a rather precise and frequently exemplary fashion.

I thought of this sentence many times as I was getting my hair cut in Berlin. And as I continued to distract myself from my ever worsening visage in the mirror in front of me with stories of that other German hairdresser, his business now modestly flourishing within the vibrant subcultures of forties or fifties New York, cutting polka dots into women's heads and shaving off only half of men's beards, I thought that perhaps all of my stories, my writings, my so-called works of literature, were exactly like this one: little tales to distract myself from something I actually didn't want to look at too closely within the strictures of the present moment. Often through conjuring up something far more confusing or worse.

Such as our sepia-toned German hairdresser arriving at his small shop on 31st Street early one morning to find a note taped to his front door. The note said:

> There is no trick to it. Nonetheless we have become aware of your activities. Perhaps you might wish to become acquainted with ours.

That was all. No names, no other information whatsoever. He tore the note from the door and stuffed it into his pocket, not giving it any real attention, though later he could not understand how he had managed to put the matter out of his mind so easily.

That morning was free of appointments, since his particular clientele were certainly not early risers, and as he sat alone in the empty shop, cleaning the scissors and mirrors he had neglected to clean the night before, gradually he did in fact find himself pondering the note, especially that first line: There was no trick to *what*? It meant nothing to him and yet, searching back through his memory he couldn't feel completely sure it didn't remind him of something. His thoughts rolled back to Germany, his formative years, when war was looming and his only option was to get out of the country as quickly as possible.

There were a few friends around at that time, certainly not close friends, who were rumoured to have gone underground. And perhaps he now remembered something, a vague recollection of sitting in some Berlin café and asking one of them what exactly it meant to 'go underground,' and then a more concrete recollection of being startled by the reply: "There's no trick to it," the words filtered back through his memory. "You simply disappear."

Then he too had disappeared, found himself here, running this strange little shop, his still thick accent a mark of authenticity among his customers who would have been just as convinced if his accent had been fake. He had survived while many others had not, though often his survival seemed to him little more than a joke. Was he anything more than a clown to these people: the mysterious, eccentric foreigner doling out stupid haircuts with a grave composure and solemn expression?

Soon the afternoon appointments would begin. At 1 p.m. he would cut the hair of a young painter from the Netherlands, in residence in New York for the last three years and probably still living off parental dosh. The rich, and what's worse the pseudo-bohemian offspring of the rich, disgusted him completely and on occasion he felt frustrated that he was in no position to turn down their money. Working for a living – he thought to himself as he began to sharpen his scissors – in fact work itself, was like a biblical plague.

The door opened behind him, the bell that hung off the doorframe tinkling as it was supposed to (he was a traditionalist in such matters) and as he turned, for a brief moment he expected to see not the young pretentious Dutch painter, who was in fact standing there with a big stupid grin on his big stupid face, but instead someone else, someone from his past he at this moment could not quite recall. The young painter, wearing the horrible purple blazer he always had on (to seem more artistic, I suppose, our German hairdresser scowled silently to himself) confidently walked over to the chair and sat down.

"Do your thing," the painter said, smiling, with a little manufactured wave of his hands. "Whatever you like. I hope you're feeling inspired today."

He was feeling inspired. Inspired to stab this moron in the

neck with his newly sharpened scissors. And to keep stabbing and twisting, and whatever other gestures might be necessary, until the moron was dead and they were both completely covered in blood. He glanced over at the window. It was a bright, sunny day. There was much street traffic. He was not a murderer and what's more he was definitely not stupid enough to commit a murder in front of a street full of happy witnesses. He was a foreigner, a German, in the eyes of everyone here probably little more than a Nazi. It must feel good to have a talented, eccentric Nazi cut your hair, a mark of artistic openness, bravery and authenticity. He hated these tepid assholes, complete wastes of flesh one and all, he thought to himself as he reached for his clippers and began to shave a bald stripe vertically across the head of the little Dutch twit.

He held the mirror vertical to the back of the twit's head, which his scissors had in fact not touched, and then angled it to each side. The bald stripe was clean and precise, very German he thought to himself, as he detached the plastic cover, shaking it out with a slight flourish.

"Are you done?" the twit seemed pleased but confused, if there was more to come he definitely wanted everything he could get.

"Of course."

"Fantastic," the twit smiled that smug smile his parents had instilled in him, stood up and casually brushed himself off. "You've once again outdone yourself." He was examining himself in the mirror, turning to one side then the other.

"Thank you," our protagonist said, trying not to let his distain feel too obvious, taking the money and folding it neatly into his modest billfold.

Later that night, as he was closing up, he once again glanced at the note (which he had now taped to the top corner of the large mirror):

> There is no trick to it. Nonetheless we have become aware of your activities. Perhaps you might wish to become acquainted with ours.

He knew these people. He remembered them vaguely but with all of the detail washed away, like a barely remembered dream. Did he in fact wish to become acquainted with their activities? He felt as if he could guess what such activities were but, upon closer inspection of his own thoughts, realized he could not. He had rushed through the last few clients on autopilot, making the usual awkward interventions in their appearance, and felt relieved when it was finally time to close shop.

And as he was leaving I was also leaving, paying the real Berlin hairdresser and feeling him scowl at me as he took my money and folded it into his pocket. "Are you from America?" he asked. "No, Canada," I replied, and in his polite nod of recognition I could hear him thinking that there was basically no difference (a sentiment I of course, at times, shared).

I left the shop and made my way down Torstr. I had no plans for the rest of the day. The haircut was it, and had been a relative disaster. As I walked I could catch an occasional glimpse of myself in the shop windows. My hair looked terrible but when did I start worrying about such things. No, I didn't give a shit about the haircut, it was only a stand-in for the fact that I was here wandering aimlessly through the streets of Berlin along with thousands of other Canadians, Danes, Swedes,

Americans, Mexicans, Norwegians, artists from every country you could possibly name, and we all wanted something from this place. Berlin was a kind of signifier, evidence we were searching for the next (or more accurately last) exciting moment, some sort of zeitgeist or locus, in our otherwise grievously dull and tepid times. Somehow, in that moment, my haircut seemed like the deflating, other-side-of-the-coin hangover to this earlier, first adventurous impulse to search.

And as I walked, perhaps a bit too aimlessly, or only too obvious in my gentle aimlessness, I continued to wonder about our future-forward German haircutter in New York. How he went home that night, fixed himself his usual simple meal, sat in his kitchen wondering about the note. It would have been immediately obvious to someone more self-aware, but it took him a while to realize that he wouldn't be thinking about it quite so much if he didn't want to know more. Would there be another note tomorrow, featuring a more elaborate hint? Or would he have to figure out the next step himself? All the things from that time in his life were completely gone. He had left with nothing but the clothes on his back in order to smoothly cross the unmanned stretch of border to Switzerland. If he had to do it all over again he wondered if he would still have the nerve.

Slowly, as he prepared for sleep, he wondered if these haircuts he was giving were enough. When he was young he had been nothing if not precocious, bursting with potential, the one everyone thought would go furthest, burn brightest. He was of course gaining a sliver of notoriety within certain New York circles, but it barely seemed like the tasks he routinely accomplished each day – yes, with a certain degree of flair and creativity, but with no great thought or effort on his part – were worthy of his younger self. What might he have done if he had remained in Germany? Would he have written philosophy? Painted? Thrown firebombs at the parliament? He could barely recall his former aspirations. The struggle to get here in one piece, set up shop starting from practically nothing, keep the work alive until eventually it became solvent, had sapped away all such dreams. Perhaps he had never exactly known *what* he would do, had only felt the world was his oyster and someday he would do something truly great.

The next morning, as he approached the shop at his usual careful pace, already he could see the note, placed in exactly the same spot as the day before. Just to show off, but in fact showing off to no one since there was no one in sight, he pulled the note off the door and crumpled it down into his pocket without even so much as glancing at it. His curiosity could wait for later. What was important now was discipline, that whatever else might happen he would be in charge, he would not allow the notes to exert any excess influence over his carefully balanced daily thoughts and actions.

The notes continued for many weeks and, in order to gain some perspective, and also to regain a certain degree of control, he bought a red scrapbook, pasting the notes within it, one per page, in chronological order. Flipping through this scrapbook each night before he went to bed, he searched for patterns or insights, as certain speculations became clear. These notes were being sent to him by people from his past, people he couldn't quite remember but who clearly remembered him. What's more, these people wanted something, required his assistance, and were biding their time until the right moment. He started again at the beginning of the scrapbook:

There is no trick to it. Nonetheless we have become aware of your activities. Perhaps you might wish to become acquainted with ours.

Turning the page:

It is unfashionable to speak of revolution. Much like yourself, we care little for passing fashions. The point is to make a decision and then to act.

And the next note:

What is a decision? How does it differ from flipping a coin? There is no trick to it. The difference is simply commitment.

And the next note always startled him, gave him pause, as he rushed through his memory to think who these note-senders might be:

You have cut our hair and it has grown back. Are these haircuts you give your final decision? We remember you. You had much greater promise.

But he couldn't identify them. He rolled through all the faces that had sat in his chair and none of them felt right. Of course, it occurred to him that they might be lying, since the notes were nothing if not a form of psychological warfare:

When one is young, one sees the world with a certain perspective. As one gets older, it is only natural

for one's perspective to shift. However, we are send-
ing these notes in order to question whether the
changes you have made are precisely the ones you
still require.

He tried to think back. Had he really been that much more
radical or political when he was young? What he remembered
most was a feeling of not being sure. Not being sure which way
to turn or which road was right for his life. Yet married to this
feeling of uncertainty was an urgency of pure fire – that above
all he must do something, do it fiercely and do it soon. For days
he would sit in the café and speak about what he should do, how
and why, perhaps masking his overwhelming feelings of uncertainty with a ferocious monologue of feigned overconfidence.
He would make his name and would do so soon and with flair.
And all of this seemed so long ago as he turned the page:

In your haircuts there is always a certain degree of
invention. We are also inventors. We are wondering
if you can guess or imagine just what it is we invent.

He could not. But then he did remember something, vaguely,
loosely, a conversation about science, about the connections
between science and revolution, and how visions of revolution
without a strong foundation in science were the emptiest uto-
pias of all.

A virus. He remembered it now. All those years ago there
was ongoing talk of a virus. A virus that would attack only the
Brownshirts and leave his leftist friends unscathed. The realization that the road to revolution lay not in the streets but in the
science labs. And yes, how could he have forgotten, but then

again he barely knew them. There were a few men and women who decided, all together, to study science, to apply themselves with the utmost seriousness: biology, pathogens.

He put aside the red scrapbook. It was time to sleep now; his memory-jogging experiment had worked, he now had a viable theory as to who was behind the notes. But had their experiment, their brave but insane notion, worked just as well?

The next day, as he arrived at the door of his small shop, he was surprised to find no note. There had been a note every day for the past three weeks and now suddenly there was none. It was as if by cracking the code, by recalling the possible identity of his note-writing tormentors, he had somehow brought the game to a close. There were no notes any day that week and no notes the week after. He was equally surprised to discover how much he missed them.

But then, near the end of the second noteless week, something happened. It was his third appointment of the afternoon, shaving one half of the head and leaving the other untouched, staring at the client's face in the mirror so intently he barely noticed the motion of his own scissors. The client was about his own age, with sharp eyes and features, and the more intently he fixated on the mirror the more he wondered if this was some face from his past.

He rarely made small talk with clients, found himself searching for precisely the right leading question, the answer to which would let him know whether he was on the right track (without giving too much away.) He'd never liked playing games, preferred the freedom of a direct approach, still wondering, as the haircut neared completion, how direct should he be? What did he actually want to know?

The man with sharp features stood up, brushed himself off,

paid in cash, added a healthy tip and left. Our German hair-dresser began to sweep up, but quickly changed his mind, closed shop, headed down the street in the direction he thought he'd seen his last client turn. (Later, when the rest of the day's clients complained they had come for their regular appointments but found the door locked, he would try to convince them that their understanding of a 'haircut' was too narrow, that they should open their minds, that the fact they had shown up to a locked shop, the frustration and confusion they had for a split second felt, was itself a kind of 'haircut,' an experience on the very cutting edge of the international conception of the profession.)

He caught sight of his client at the end of the street and walked steadily in pursuit. In the past, his desire had always been to flee from his clients. This was the first time he had ever found himself on the chase. But as he thought this he realized he still had the desire to flee, was in pursuit almost in spite of himself, or perhaps only in spite of his current self, drifting back to former days when he would often display such random, ill-conceived bursts of curiosity or courage.

The man with sharp features turned a corner and our German hairdresser quickened his pace so as not to lose him. It was impossible to follow someone, to follow a complete stranger, without feeling oneself to be a character from cinema, some sort of thriller, without hearing the imaginary string section start to build as one's step quickened. He deplored the way cinema had corrupted even his imagination, he who had watched so little and thought even less of the few films he had seen. Up ahead the man with sharp features turned into a building and our German hairdresser stopped just outside the door, the imaginary string section stopping cold along with him.

He had no idea what to do, standing there, wondering if he should go in or wait outside. He wasn't sure why he remembered this, but he had passed this place every day on his way to the shop, and someone, perhaps a client, had once told him they called it 'headquarters,' headquarters of some awful, rapacious multinational that did all the normal, awful multinational kinds of things, keeping the world turning and unfair. He stared at the building, at its front doors, wondering for a moment how it worked inside, still wondering if he should go in, waiting for something to happen.

And then something did: A woman careened out the front doors, ran past him, chased by two security guards, and without thinking, without taking even a moment to contemplate, he leapt onto the security guards, miraculously managing to trip one, toppling on top of the other. If there had still been violins in his head they would have really been going for it now, but there was nothing, only the brute instincts of survival. He reached for the gun still in the outstretched hand of the guard underneath him, rolling the guard on top to use as a shield if the other were to start shooting, a fist hit his face, and trying to protect himself with his elbows as both hands grappled for the outstretched gun, managed to wrench it free, pulled himself out from under the man punching him, sat up and pointed the gun, first at one guard, then at the other, then back at the first. A standstill.

It was at this moment that the guards both realized their main task was not to fight with this complete stranger but to chase after the woman who had just had sex with their boss. "We should keep chasing that girl," one of them mumbled, and they were off. Our German hairdresser noticed he was standing in a public place holding a gun and quickly shoved it into his jacket pocket.

The next day, as he arrived at the shop, he was once again disappointed to realize there was no note. For a moment that morning, he had considered putting on sunglasses to conceal his very swollen left eye (the right one wasn't much better), but he didn't own sunglasses, and as he walked to work it occurred to him that two black eyes would only serve to increase his mystique, increase his appeal to a clientele that loved everything strange, debased or out of the ordinary.

His clients that day were the usual idiots, each one asking about his shiner, expressing feigned curiosity and fake concern. He was in a pissy mood, all the small talk about the state of his face only increasing his scorn for this series of completely American morons, and he did everything in his power to give each the stupidest haircut possible, for which they thanked him effusively, a few even seeming somewhat genuine as they did so.

Near the end of the day, when all of his scheduled appointments were done and he was thinking of closing up early, a woman came in, the same woman who had run past him as she was bursting out of headquarters, who he now, for a brief moment, felt almost heroic for having rescued from the two security guards. (He had the black eyes to prove it.)

"This might sound strange," she said, "but I don't actually want my hair cut. I just want you to pretend to cut my hair. Keep up appearances."

He stared at her in the mirror as she continued.

"If you take off a few split ends I suppose it won't do any

harm, but when I leave this chair I want my hair to look exactly the same."

He nodded brusquely in agreement, as if he understood when actually he did not, and immediately got down to work, snipping away just millimetres from her head, only rarely touching her hair.

After a long period of silent snipping, during which practically no hair was cut, just a few wisps on the floor, she spoke again.

"I'm dying," she said.

"Oh," our hairdresser replied blankly.

As she spoke she often hesitated. There were pauses during which he believed she had finished until, eventually, she continued.

"There's a virus. For political reasons I believed it should be spread. And it is being spread. But, as well, it's killing me. Slowly. Not so slowly. I don't really know. Do you understand?"

"Perhaps," our German replied, not wanting to give anything away.

"Normally I wouldn't mind. I think it's a beautiful thing to die for a cause one believes in. But something happened. One year ago. I fell in love with a woman. We live together. And now suddenly I do mind. Love makes you want to live. Squeeze every last drop out of life. Now suddenly I want to live again. And it's too late."

Our German put down the scissors. There was no clear ending to a job in which no hair was cut and he decided now was as good a time as any to stop. It had been a short one, but his sessions were often quite brief. He reached for the broom out of habit, to sweep up, even though there was nothing to sweep.

"And from your perspective," he said, "all of this has something to do with me?"

That night she took him to a meeting. At the meeting was the client he had followed the previous day, a few other Germans about his age all looking vaguely familiar, plus a few younger members, concentrated young men ready to prove themselves. The woman he had rescued from the security guards sat directly to his left. She refused to give her name so he decided to call her Claire.

Claire looked over at him. "We don't bring anyone here. Not anymore. There's been some trouble lately: infighting, assassinations."

Our German was doing his best to remain impassive but he could feel his interest growing. "You don't bring anyone here?"

"No."

"So why did you bring me?"

"We invited you because we are hoping you have a second idea."

"What was my first idea?"

There was a sharp silence. Everyone stared at him as if he was a complete idiot, as if they were waiting for him to correct an imponderable gaffe. The previous day's client cut in: "Your first idea was the virus."

They had to explain carefully. They all knew the details backwards and forwards, but, though the story primarily concerned him, he had only the vaguest memory.

It was in the café twenty years ago, the café he went to every morning, where he would talk to anyone that would listen, where he held court. (Though there were so many other young men in the same café holding court as well.) He had been pontificating on the various struggles of the current Left, how the Fascists were gaining ground while the left seemed to lose every battle. He was wondering what it might mean to change the battlefield, to find territory more conducive to their progressive goals. Because on the streets fear, intimidation and mob politics won out every time. It was so much easier to prey on what was worst in people, and to make considerable use of it, than to call upon the masses to raise themselves up, make of themselves something better. The streets were dirty, harsh – a foul joke or swift kick in the groin would win out every time. Where was the territory in which some nobler tactics might prevail? He was speculating that perhaps it was on a more basic level, on the level of cells, of genes, riffing off of a variety of self-taught morsels from biology, physics, phrenology. A virus isn't swayed by propaganda, he had said. A virus finds its true course and follows it to the end. That was the phrase that had clicked, that they locked onto. They all remembered it, even the ones who hadn't been there. It is what they believed they were doing to this day. Finding the true course and following it to the end.

That night they took him to the orgy. Dishevelled clothing and half-naked bodies spread out like a carpet in front of him. He couldn't imagine how an offhand comment made twenty years ago could have led to all this. He walked slowly through the room and watched the businessmen fucking, in various positions and with varying degrees of detachment and passion, wondering if he too might soon be similarly entangled or if he would continue to simply watch. Claire came up beside him, took his hand and led him to a corner where they started to make out. "This is a test," she whispered in his ear, "an initiation. I have the virus. If we fuck and you manage to avoid it, that means we can trust you." He froze as she continued to kiss him. It had been a long time since he had considered himself part of the genuine Left, or part of anything for that matter, anything other than his own idiosyncratic path. He pulled away and looked at her. She looked back at him with neither desire nor judgment. "Let me look around first," he said. "You don't gamble your life without knowing the house." Turning away he was filled with a strange surge of desire.

When I write about sex, I always feel like someone who has never had sex writing about sex, so distant is my experience from the words I am able to get down. I have often felt that I should try to remedy this dilemma, to write my actual, emotional experience of sex, as accurately as possible, but it seems beyond my abilities, the nuances too paradoxical and complex, too many emotions and desires conflicting in too many ways. Or perhaps it is only shame that stops me. I believe I experience a low-level lust towards basically every woman I see. This isn't so unusual, but it constitutes the background, the pulse of subconscious daily dissatisfaction that informs any experience I might have of actual sex. I do not believe sex is normal or natural. It seems rare and strange, a momentary exception amongst a vast expanse of unrelated, yet intensely related, activities. I've never been in love and I don't play any sports. I've once again failed in my attempts at description, failed to even begin, and I don't know why anyone would want to read this paragraph. Then again, on the part of the reader there is often a considerable desire to learn biographical information about the neuroses of the writer.

Our German hairdresser wandered through the orgy with the implacable gaze of a true voyeur. He thought back to earlier in the evening, at the meeting, how they had carefully explained the virus to him, many technical details he didn't catch or comprehend. "There is no way to fight against this world using reason or action alone," they had explained. "The virus goes beyond reason, beyond action. In that sense it is more pure, more natural. If we'd had this in 1933, the Holocaust might have never happened." He didn't understand why they were trying to convince him. If it had originally been his idea, shouldn't he be trying to convince them? In one sense they were only clarifying the landscape, giving him a picture of where he currently stood, but in another sense it was like, without knowing it, they were seeking approval from Daddy, seeking his permission. In front of him on a small pile of mattresses three naked men and two naked women had their fingers, tongues, teeth and fluids prodding, biting, spilling everywhere. He stood and watched, surprised at the degree to which he didn't feel aroused, wondering what exactly it was he did feel: somewhat curious and mainly nothing. This is how we kill the rich, he wondered to himself. This is the honey that sets the trap?

I will try again. At first all I feel is the desire to be close, to feel the warmth of another body pressed against my own. Already I know that within me there exists much more desire than this simple, rather sweet, need for contact, but in the first moments it is all I am able to access. Yet as soon as there is contact the arousal kicks in, an intensity, hard and fast, throwing me off, striking me off-kilter as if I hadn't been expecting it, a confusion. I know I want something but I don't know what. I bite, lick, struggle, caress and stroke. My fingers want to go everywhere. If my partner seems excited by something I do then I do it more, if she is excited then my excitement grows out from hers like a vampire seeking energy. I am hard and soft and hard again and it seems to make no difference. I want to go forever but I don't know where. I feel tired, sad and excited. My body is doing one thing and my mind is wondering why, starting to become bored, thinking I should end the relationship before it becomes too serious, starting to think about other things, almost coming but feeling its too soon so pulling away, disengaged but pulsing everywhere until, a few rounds later, I come, a small sudden jolt, and completely collapse. In less than one second, sex and my partner are the furthest things from my mind, and there is a certain degree of guilt I feel almost too exhausted to access.

"What kind of second idea are you looking for," he had asked the gathering. It was not a rhetorical question. He was genuinely engaged, curious in a way he couldn't remember having been for a very long time.

"We were hoping you could tell us."

"I'm not sure I have ideas like that anymore." He was thinking back, questioning everything, questioning himself. "Now I give haircuts." But even as he said this, ideas began storming through his head, ideas that had nothing to do with haircuts or the way his life was today, his thoughts from twenty years ago rushing into the present. Because, it now seemed to him, the right wing he was wondering how to fight all those years ago – the Fascists, the Brownshirts – were not the same as the right wing today. These days it had more to do with business, money, religion. What if you were to fight fire with fire, money with money, belief with belief? Would it be possible to get rich in some way that, at the same time, could decimate the Right, disgrace power? To form a religion that could undermine their strength? What business plan, what church, could set the foundations for such an attack? And as he was struck by such thoughts he realized he was speaking them aloud, without meaning to, all it took was an audience, a request, and off he went. "A church that is also a business. Because religion is like a fantasy, a dream, and maybe money is also a kind of fantasy, they belong together. So then a religion in the form of a dream that hurtles forward towards the future, because money is energy stored away for what comes next, but also a dream for now, because there's no living without cash. A dream for the future and a dream for now. A religion-business hybrid. A structure that people could believe in the same way they believe in God, that would at the same time ferment their resistance. That would bind together the worldly, unfightable love of money with the timeless need to believe in something, wrap it all up into a functional leftist package, shifting the balance between Left and Right."

And one of those young men at the table, listening as intently as the rest, didn't yet know it but someday he would end up back home, make a pact with his friends to all write books with the exact same title, in fact he would provide the title himself, not even realizing from precisely where in his subconscious it had come. But all that was still in the future, not yet happening, not even the kernel of a dream as the others continued to listen and our hairdresser startled forward on the charge of his own improvised thoughts. "It could start with a miracle. People always need a miracle to get them going. But forward from the miracle you could slowly weave in the traditional discourse of the Left, of equality, of new models for living, of questioning the economy, of questioning power. Because the religion that the Right is pushing, with or without sincerity, that religion happened thousands of years ago. Maybe we could take them if our religion was in the present, something happening right now."

He had them, everyone at the table clicking on his every word, and at the same time he barely knew what he was saying, had no idea if his words made sense, or even what sense might mean in such a situation. Did he really believe it was possible to start a credible religion today? But it was no more far-fetched than the virus, and it now seemed the virus was in full effect. Already the questions were coming at him, everyone throwing them faster than he could consider.

"But this business-religion model, how would it be different from the religions that already exist? What's the point of replacing one evil with its reflection?"

He had no idea but there was no stopping him: "That's the challenge we have to set for ourselves."

"Something pointless, something redundant, is not a challenge."

"Trying to change people, really change them, their perceptions, change them on the most fundamental level, that's not redundant. That's possibly the most difficult and valuable thing one can attempt."

"Stringing people along on the leash of religion, are you sure that's going to change them in some fundamental way?"

"I'm not sure about anything. I didn't ask to be brought here. Twenty years ago I said some things, said some things and never thought twice about them. It's you who gave importance to what I had said, and here again, all of you, have to decide whether to give any importance to what I'm saying now. Tomorrow I'll still wake up, wander to my shop as I have done every day for years, and cut some people's hair. You asked me for an idea and I've given you one."

"We're just trying to understand."

"You're not trying to understand. You're taking turns, you're attacking me."

Had they really been attacking him? He didn't know. Maybe he was only too sensitive, not as tough as he'd been in former days. He continued to drift silently through the orgy, thinking back again and again to the spontaneous proposals and arguments he had made only a few hours ago, spectacular yet dull pleasures surrounding him on all sides.

He looked up. There was a large metal cage swaying a few feet above his head. From where he stood he could only see the underside of its metal floor, could not see what was happening within, but the swaying of the cage was clearly fucking. In fact, everywhere was fucking, there was no need to guess. He calmly retraced his steps, making his way back to Claire, new lust growing with every step. Claire lay on a couch by the front door. He sat down beside her. She was there to give him the initiation. She was waiting.

"Are you really dying?"

"Yes."

"It's strange. Maybe I don't know what to believe any more. I don't quite believe you."

"Belief has nothing to do with it."

He wasn't sure. He thought: If you believe you are going to live then perhaps you live and if you think you're going to die then your chances grow slimmer. He wanted to say this, convince her, throw in his vote of confidence, but was too afraid. She would think him mystical, just another boring mystic wanting to start a religion and con the masses. Instead he reached over, looking into her eyes for permission as he did so, slowly sliding his hand up into her skirt. He was again about to speak, not sure what to say but wanting to say something, not do this only in silence, but she gave a shiver of pleasure, pushed her hips up into his palm and all thoughts, all words, fled from his mind. Through her underwear he could feel she was wet, softly starting to grind, pushing the wetness up into his palm. He remembered back at the shop she had told him she was in love with someone else, a woman, that falling in love had made her want to live. She slid her legs around him, wrapping him in a tightened embrace, scratching her short nails through the back of his hair. Suddenly this is what he wanted more than anything and if he died he couldn't care less. He wondered if he would ever fall in love, thought that soon it would be too late. They were real revolutionaries, Claire and the rest. Did he care about revolution? He was impressed by how much they'd accomplished, how hard they'd fought, but looking into their future he saw only failure. She was undoing his belt, his pants, as she kissed him, biting at the edge of his lips, licking his cheek up toward his eye, her teeth dragging lightly over his ear and back down his neck. There was fumbling, his pants, his underwear, awkwardly down over his ankles, propping himself up on one elbow, a slight discomfort and, suddenly, he was inside her. She bit his shoulder hard, straight through his shirt, as with one hand he eased off the rest of her clothes, his other arm wrapped tightly around her back, keeping her close. Why was she doing this? he wondered. But she was a revolutionary, part of a secret society, and in revolution you do what you must. They were two people fucking in a room full of the same. He kissed her and she licked and held his mouth, pressed against him for everything he was worth, new moans, purrs and grunts with every off-balance thrust. His mind was both here and elsewhere, still thinking back to the meeting, how the questions had continued, confused him, growing harsher and more critical, as if they'd brought him to the meeting not for his ideas but to debate. She pressed her thumb into his asshole as he rolled on top.

"You can say my plan for a religion is unethical. But I could just as easily turn it around: What's so ethical about a virus? I thought the point was to win."

"With the virus, we're killing only our enemies. Our friends remain free. With a religion, you're manipulating friends and enemies alike, manipulating people we hope will someday march alongside us. You're coercing them, taking away their free will."

"But the main people we'd be manipulating aren't our friends. It's by manipulating them we can turn them into friends. Convert them to the cause."

For a moment he thought he was going to come, but didn't. He pulled out and slid his face down between her legs, licking and sucking, short little licks, his hands clenching her ass, barely able to breath but wanting nothing else but to lick and feel her tremble, still thinking back, unable to bring his mind into the present. They had been looking for a fight, considered him, as the unintentional founder of their endeavour, the most worthy, but also most difficult, adversary.

"We're trying to move towards a world in which subjecting people, manipulating them, becomes a thing of the past. You can't use poison to cure the disease."

"You can in a homeopathic dose."

"Starting a world religion doesn't sound like homeopathy. It sounds more like surgery, like a heart transplant, like replacing the heart of their business and religion with the heart of ours."

"But you're killing people. There must be an ethical argument that converting them is better than killing them."

"It just depends on what kind of life you think is, and isn't, worth living. Conversion is another kind of death."

He could see they had been through all this before, had worked every angle, while he was thinking everything for the first time. Someone who has never had sex writing about sex. Someone who has never killed or fought writing about violence. He scrambled back up her body, thrusting his hips downwards as his lips met her neck. The moment he was inside he again feared he might come, and slowing down, clinging to her, tighter and tighter, everything moving more slowly now, tried to silently pull her into his thoughts of the meeting that was still only a few hours ago.

"But then who are you to decide?"

"As you said twenty years ago, we have found our true course and are following it through to the end."

"I wasn't talking about people, I was talking about viruses."

"That is the beauty of our group: We have taken biology, the virus, as our model."

"And then how many people do you plan to kill?"

"We don't think of our project in terms of numbers. We think only of following things through until the end."

"Let's say I wanted to think of it in numbers."

"If the virus kills half of the planet, more than half of the planet, that's simply a step along the path. The people who are left will be the good ones, can start again, will be the people who can begin to build a more realistic, a more constructive, a better, world. What we destroy opens up possibilities that humanity has never dreamt of. How can you put a price on such a thing?"

The frightening thing is everyone has their reasons.

7. The Fascist Now

Early in 2002 there was a rumour: that while on his way to attend the New York Film Festival, the internationally acclaimed Iranian filmmaker Abbas Kiarostami was denied entry to the United States, presumably because, for them, everyone from that part of the world was the same and therefore a potential terrorist. This rumour was true and, at the time, seemed to me absolute evidence that, post-9/11, the United States had gone completely to hell. (As we know, endless waves of further evidence were to come.)

Early in 2002 Kiarostami still represented something for me, as if he was the last man standing, the last in a long line of untarnished art-house cinema auteurs. It seemed to me, from reading about it in magazines and newspaper articles, that the Tehran cinema of the nineties was a situation comparable to Paris in the sixties – a new wave of cinematic ingenuity, freely mixing documentary and artistic rigour.

What I did not yet know was that at that same 2002 New York Film Festival, Filmmaker A, still a young woman, long before any thoughts of new filmmaking had crossed her mind, was premiering her first feature, a slice-of-life drama about a group of young anarchists living in a shared home in Arizona, a sly mixture of fiction and documentary that skilfully used non-actors, genuine young anarchists, for its cast.

Along with Kiarostami, the Iranian New Wave included the filmmakers Jafar Panahi, Majid Majidi, Bahram Beizai, Dariush Mehrjui, Mohsen Makhmalbaf, Masoud Kimiai, Sohrab Shahid-Saless, Parviz Kimiavi, Samira Makhmalbaf, Amir Naderi and Abolfazl Jalili. Most of these names mean nothing to me, except for two. Jafar Panahi, often described as 'Kiarostami's disciple,' who came to my attention when in 2010 he was arrested and jailed (he was released three months later). And Mohsen Makhmalbaf who is the narrative linchpin in Kiarostami's film *Close-Up*, the film that meant the most to me over the course of the nineties, and also the film that Filmmaker A first saw by him, raising so many questions within her. This was the film that led her to want to meet Kiarostami at the New York Film Festival, a desire of course thwarted by his non-arrival.

In a review from 1999, the film critic Godfrey Cheshire writes: "An unusual mixture of found reality and fictional elaboration, *Close-Up* documents the case of Hossein Sabzian, the Makhmalbaf impersonator. The film began with a story in the Tehran weekly *Sorush*, which said that a man had been arrested for pretending to be Mohsen Makhmalbaf, one of Iran's most famous film directors, to a middle-class family. The ruse apparently was somewhat innocent at first. The family, the Ahankhahs, invited the supposed Makhmalbaf into their home after the wife met him on a bus. He regaled them with tales of his career and offered to put them in his next film. But the deception soon began to unravel. 'Makhmalbaf' didn't know anything about an international award the papers said he had won. More crucially, he borrowed money from the family and didn't return it. Suspecting they were being set up for a bigger rip-off, Mr. Ahankhah contacted the authorities."

In July 2010 I sent the following email to a handful of people:

Dear _____,

I'm currently in this one-month writing residency just outside of Viborg, Denmark, in the middle of Danish nature. There are green rolling hills, sheep and cows, and an amazingly placid lake. There is absolutely nothing to do here and it is very, very quiet. I am here with a writer from Uganda, one from Italy, one from NY, plus a few from Denmark (who rotate).

I am working on a new novel entitled *Artists Are Self-Absorbed*. [Later the title was changed to *Polyamorous Love Song*.] I didn't mean it to happen, but somehow Abbas Kiarostami has become a character within the book, in and around his film *Close-Up*, how it plays with the boundary between reality and fiction. Also how *Close-Up* seems to be extremely different from any of his other films and what that might mean.

So I thought I would send a question to a handful of people who might have some thoughts. Don't feel in any way obligated, but I was wondering if you have any stories about, or insights into, Kiarostami, *Close-Up* or Mohsen Makhmalbaf? Or if they mean anything in particular to you?

Very much hope all is well.
Jacob

The first reply came almost immediately. It was from someone I didn't know, who I stumbled upon on the internet around the same time I was composing the above email, a complete stranger living somewhere in Iran.

To tell you the truth, I'm not that familiar with Kiarostami or Makhmalbaf, it is ages that they do not live in Iran and their movies are not shown in Iran, because of our totalitarian regime. Censoring their movies and political reasons were the cause of their immigration to other countries. I am not a fan of Persian cinema, but your message motivated me to go and watch their movies, especially Kiarostami. Thanks and sorry that I couldn't help you. Wish you luck and success.

Filmmaker A turned twenty-six in the summer of 2002. She was excited she had made her first feature before turning thirty, and that it had already been accepted at such a prestigious festival. She was thinking so much about how to use real people, real life, in her films. What were the repercussions and ethics of using non-actors, their stories, their improvisations? To what degree did she want to take the things they said and did and shape them, script them, make their stories into her own works of art, and to what degree did she want to let things stand, to cut the material into her story unaltered, into a narrative she would create in and around it? When she shaped the material more, it sometimes felt like she was betraying the very performers who had been so generous with their time and ideas, that she was twisting the semi-improvised scenes so they were no longer recognizable to those who cared most about them. But when she used the material unaltered, it was as if she wasn't doing her job, she might as well leave the set and let them make the film themselves – a more politically radical move but possibly less strong on an artistic level.

The next response I got was from the Iranian playwright and theatre director Amir Reza Koohestani.

I am very much interested in your project and will be more than happy to help . . .

I personally met Kiarostami twice, as he was supposed to adapt one of my plays, *Dance on Glasses,* for cinema. We met in the hotel in Brussels during the Kunsten Festival 2004 and then in Tehran. That project never happened, because of so many different reasons, although we are still following each other's works. Accidentally, I am writing a film script for Mani Haghighi based on Kiarostami's plot. So we talk a lot about Kiarostami's cinema and his manifest. Besides, I am a fan of *Close-Up,* so don't hesitate to write to me any further questions.

In New York that year, when people would speak to Filmmaker A about her film, it seemed they always wanted to know the same thing: How much of it was real and how much was invented? And Filmmaker A couldn't tell them, either because she couldn't remember or because answering such a question in anything resembling a direct manner felt like a betrayal of some sort. A betrayal of the spontaneity of the adaptations, of the porous barriers between reality and fiction that wrapped around and weaved through every day of the shoot and edit.

At the same festival there was a German film, I believe it

might have even won a prize, about the years leading up to World War Two. It covered the slow rise of Fascism and how powerless those who were against it felt, how difficult it seemed to do anything to stem the tide. Filmmaker A watched the film at the gala along with everyone else, and as she watched all she could think was: They wouldn't let Kiarostami into the country, they're interring 'suspected terrorists' in camps, it's just like what happened in Germany, just like this fucking boring film, the same thing is happening here. The film was well made, clean and sleek, and as the young intellectual protagonists watched the Nazi parades, the music swelled ominously to indicate that the noose was tightening.

The German intellectuals – each played with panache by photogenic, most likely ambitious, young actors – had endless conversations, fretting about strategy, about what could be done, conversations in bars, smoke-filled coffee shops and on the street, until the climactic scene in which the male and female leads, who, without realizing, had gradually fallen in love over the course of the film, smuggle a group of Jewish children over the border into Switzerland. A happy ending to Nazism. Just on the other side, they stand in the frame of a panoramic shot, dawn softly breaking in the background behind them, and discuss whether to stay in Switzerland or return to the struggle back home. She decides to stay. His conscience won't let him live in peace while others – friends, relatives and strangers – are in such overwhelming danger. Music swells over the closing credits as a futile quest for justice takes precedence over new love. This is bullshit, Filmmaker A thought under her breath, this isn't the cinema we need.

It was also sometime around 2002, or perhaps just after, that I read the following on the internet, written by Terry Tempest

Williams in response to a friend asking if she was out of jail yet.

Dearest Bert:

Yes, I am out of jail. And here we are hours from war. I appreciated receiving the *NY Times* editorial. You are right, it articulates perfectly our feelings. On Saturday, there was the "Code Pink" Rally at Martin Luther King Park. I honestly cannot articulate the power of that day. We walked four miles or so to Lafayette Park directly across from The White House only to find a blockade of police dressed in black, bullet proof vests, rifles, clubs – standing shoulder to shoulder. We were not allowed to enter the park, this park that is a public park, this park I had just sat in hours before, this park where "Pro-life demonstrators" were standing in with their hideous, brutal pictures. They were standing in front of The White House – where we could not. We tried to negotiate with the police. It was clear they could barely uphold the law they were being asked to enforce. We made the decision that 25 of us would test the waters . . . Rachel Bagby, one of the most powerful, beautiful African American women, began singing with the strength of her voice (her voice is legendary). She began singing, "All we are saying . . . is give peace a chance." She would not stop. We joined her, thousands of women joined in this song. Her eyes locked on the African American policeman blocking her. His eyes met hers . . . and in that moment, you could see the instant recognition that both of them were there because of dissent, the dissent of their mothers and fathers before them. He quietly stepped to the side and created an opening, the opening we walked through. This is how I remember it. Once "inside" we walked toward the White House, now prohibited. Slowly, incrementally, we just kept walking backwards, singing, quietly, peacefully. The police said our arrest was imminent. That at 4:05 p.m. they would begin the arrests if we did not leave. 4:05 came, 4:10, 4:20 – We had managed to simply be there, as people have always been allowed to be there before all this "Homeland Security." The local captain of the police said he was not going to arrest us. He then asked Nina Utne, in a whisper, if he could have a Code Pink button for his wife. The atmosphere changed abruptly when the federal police arrived. They arrested Amy Goodman of *Democracy Now*, press – They took her camera. She was yelling, "You cannot arrest me I am press, I am protected by the First Amendment. I am bearing witness. I am not with these women." It didn't matter. They then went over and arrested a second press person, took her camera. It was only then I became frightened. We kept walking until our heels touched the White House fence. We turned and faced The White House . . . our "illegal act." Two cars arrived and wagons – the FBI police arrived, set up a tripod with a video camera and filmed us, each one of us – after they were done – the arrests began. Can I tell you what that felt like to watch Alice Walker, Maxine Hong Kingston, Susan Griffin and the Reverend Patricia (I have forgotten her last name) who had just returned from Iraq, handcuffed, photographed like criminals against a white sheet taped to the paddy wagon and taken away? Can I tell you what it felt like to be stripped of all possessions, notebook, pen, handcuffed, photographed, then yanked into the back of a dark vehicle and shoved into a make-shift cell and find yourself sitting next to Amy Goodman who almost died in Timor – and then hear the door slam shut and locked. In the back of the vehicle, we listened to these women tell their stories about what was it in their lives that brought them to this place. None of us had any intention of being arrested. And then we were taken to Anacostia Corrections Facility, booked, fingerprinted, and locked in a cell. Alice, Maxine, and I were in one cell with a brave student named Holly, 19 years old, and a wonderful housewife from Houston who told us her name was "Mrs. McWhorter." Four hours later, we were released. As Maxine said, "It was the least we could do." Forgive this long letter, but my heart is full and what can we do but tell our stories and stand on our ground, even as we go to war. I read the other day in one of the poems sent to Congress that "our personal anarchy is composed of deep pain and intense joys."

Love to you,
Terry

Abbas Kiarostami being denied entry to the United States and Terry Tempest Williams's email above: From 2002, or around that time, those are the two things I remember most. I am aware that by including such a letter I am highlighting how much better written, how much more heartfelt and concrete, it is than anything I have come up with, but I believe it is worth it. Sometimes memories can feel almost like dreams.

After watching the award-winning German film, Filmmaker A went to yet another festival party. In cocktail conversation after conversation, she rolled out her feeling that what was happening now in America was just like what happened in Germany in the years leading up to the war. She was amazed how few people agreed with her, and even those who did seemed to feel she was exaggerating. How could so many people not see? Everyone thinking one thing and you thinking the opposite of course does not guarantee you are wrong. Over time your views might still prevail. All it means is you need to fight, persuade, take the time and energy required to show the world what is what.

The next reply came from Andreas Lewin. After an introduction concerning other matters, he writes about *Close-Up*:

I think there is too much interpretation of the border between fiction and reality. More important is the relationship between lies and the truth. Kiarostami actually wanted later to make a documentary about the "criminal actor," after he was hired for other films! So they met several times again. But unfortunately Sabjan died before they started shooting . . . Also interesting is what Kiarostami said about *Close-Up*, that it is the only one of his films which he can see together with an audience, because "it wasn't my film." . . . I think many of the themes of *Close-Up* are also in his other films. And he also liked to build myths around his films . . . One can find a line from his early films until his new film *Copie conforme*, which is dealing with the relationship between original and copy. I can highly recommend the book by Jonathan Rosenbaum about Kiarostami. The book starts with a quote by Orson

Welles about theater: "I want to give the audience a hint of a scene. No more than that. Give them too much and they won't contribute anything themselves. Give them just a suggestion and you get them working with you. That's what gives the theatre meaning: when it becomes a social act."

Filmmaker A kept thinking about her film, about the cast who weren't even here for the screening, so rough in front of her camera and so generous with their time and ideas, some of whom she might, for whatever reason, never see again, and about *Close-Up*, and the fact that Kiarostami was denied entry, and somehow, in her mind, these things became intertwined. She knew soon it would be time for her to make a new film, but how could she make fiction as her country was throttling towards Fascism. And she knew it wasn't a matter of making documentaries, of shining a light on the problems, of showing people what was really happening. People didn't care what was happening. Even when they knew, it seemed too disconnected from their daily lives. She was too ambitious to give up on art and devote herself to full-time activism.

That morning she had a meeting with a distributor. He had been in the business much longer than her. She couldn't tell if he was in his late sixties or mid-seventies but, if you didn't look too closely, he could have easily passed for fifty. "I liked your film, it's refreshing," he began, probably just to break the ice or have something to say.

She hated that word – refreshing – always felt it was a backhanded compliment, playing off the incredible staleness of everything else on the market.

It was a breakfast meeting. He had ordered a cappuccino

and she was drinking a double espresso, black. They were both looking at the menu when suddenly she had one of those moments when everything on offer sickened her. All the wealth and unacknowledged sense of entitlement summed up in line after line of overstuffed, overpriced choice. What did this food mean? How could she eat these things when bombs were being dropped on children in Iraq? Every ingredient listed and tastefully described felt like poison. She could almost taste them and they tasted like ashes. She'd had a similar sensation a few times before, mainly in supermarkets, walking slowly along the aisle and for every can, box and item that surrounded her she could feel there was someone in the world who was going without. That everything flowed in only one direction: from the natural resources and labour of the poor into the shopping malls and supermarkets of the rich. She would look at her empty shopping cart and it would feel like a crime to place even a single item into it. At the same time she found such reactions absurd, a bit too much, over the top. Of course it was only a supermarket, only a rather average menu in an upscale New York brunch restaurant. But her thoughts were no less disturbing in light of their absurdity. She put the menu down.

"Maybe I'll just stick to coffee for now."

"I know you're most likely on a budget. You know that quip from Godard: Movies aren't a good way to make money, they're a good way to spend it. He was really onto something there. But breakfast is of course on me."

"No, really, it's all right. Just coffee is fine."

"Trying to prove your artistic credentials by starving yourself?" He was openly laughing at her now. He thought she was pretentious. Maybe he had already thought she was pretentious from watching her film, and her refusal of breakfast only confirmed his first impression. He continued: "All right, I'm absolutely famished, but I'll just stick to coffee as well. I hate to eat alone. What's more, I really hate to eat alone with someone watching me. Makes me incredibly self-conscious." He looked straight at her with a big shit-eating grin. "Come on, meet me halfway here. Order something small. It's my treat and my pleasure."

She opened the menu again. She had this feeling that whatever she did next would determine how the rest of their meeting would go. Maybe even whether or not he would choose to distribute her film. She felt her own youth and inexperience as she tried to decide, then smiled slyly.

"All right, have it your way. I also hate to watch a man eat alone."

The waiter was already approaching. She looked up at him.

"I'll have number eighteen. And another one of these." She lifted her cup a few inches off its saucer, at the same time keeping an eye on the distributor as he scanned to see what she had picked, the most expensive item on the menu. If she was going to feel sick, be disgusted, she wanted to feel sick and disgusted in style.

"I'll have the same," he said.

Near the end of the meeting, as they were finishing their third coffees, and her spell of consumerist disgust was now long behind her, a spell she now thought of as a panic attack triggered by the stress of having to try to sell her film, the distributor started to say some things that genuinely interested her. "People say movies are escapist, just entertainment, but I think that's only an alibi, a way of hiding from ourselves just how effective what we do actually is. When something is in a movie, and especially when something is in a particularly successful film, its language, its grammar, is added into the grammar of possible reality. The banal fact that sharks are terrifying was cemented into our cultural imagination after *Jaws*. We have no idea how much power we have and absolutely no idea how to use it. It's like we invent people's dreams."

And suddenly she realized what it was that infuriated her so much about the Kiarostami incident. They hadn't turned him away because he was important, because he was influential, because some people listened to what he said or because he was a great filmmaker. They had turned him away only because of the colour of his skin. It was like the ultimate insult. In a split second all of his work, his influence, was washed away, suddenly meant nothing. That was how stupid this administration was, they had silenced him almost by accident. And she felt in that moment that this government would eventually fail, that in the long run they would not win, and began to wonder again about the content of her next film.

The distributor was still speaking but Filmmaker A had drifted off. She pulled herself back into the room and listened. "Every film is also a documentary, because when you watch a film from fifty years ago, the costumes, the haircuts, the ways of walking and talking, the cars and buildings, all give a glimpse back into that time. Like in your film: the mix of political apathy and rage your characters have when they're watching the bombings, the shock-and-awe footage, on stolen cable. The way they're talking about it, like when the lesbian with the dreadlocks says: 'What does it mean to live in a world where, even if you've lived your entire life as an avowed pacifist, all you can think about is strangling the president with your bare hands.' I think fifty years from now that way of speaking, that way of thinking, will seem utterly of our time. That shock of transition."

"You think so much will have changed?"

"Of course things are going to change. Maybe not in fifty, maybe in a hundred years. But things are changing already. Pacifists want to strangle people for God's sake."

"Pacifists have always wanted to strangle people. If you didn't want to strangle someone there would be no point in calling yourself a pacifist. That's why you make the decision in the first place, to give some ideological counterweight against your natural urge for violence."

"I don't think that's why people become pacifists. I think it's more of a strategy. Because if you stick to the road of pacifism then, whatever happens, you can always claim the true moral high ground. And on moral high ground you might hit an impasse, but you will never face an absolute dead end. You can always say, on questions of strategy at least, we were right, we were pure. It keeps the battle open indefinitely. If the enemy is wrong and you are right then there will always be someone new to take up the mantle."

"I heard that in Tibet now the younger monks want to take up arms."

"That's what I said before. Things are changing."

She thought about this. She couldn't tell if things were changing, and if they were, she felt they were only changing for the worse. Was the world becoming a more violent place as she sat here digesting Eggs Benedict and being entertained by the theories of an older, more successful crank? The world had always been violent. But there is 'always,' there is history, and then there is one's own immediate lifetime. Maybe for the first time in her life she was witnessing, she was about to witness, a real increase in the bloodshed of the world. She didn't know. Predicting the future was a sucker's game. Anything might happen.

Godfrey Cheshire writes: "*Close-Up* invites endless interpretation, but Kiarostami is clear about his reading of it. He says it is about the power of imagination, and of cinema as a vehicle of dreams. As he put it to me: 'With the help of dreams you can escape from the worst prisons. Actually, you can only imprison the body but dreams flee the walls and without visas or dollars can travel anywhere. In dreams, you can sleep with anyone you want. Nobody can touch your dreams. In a way dreams exactly embody the concept of freedom. They free you of all constraints. I think God gave human beings this possibility to apologize for all the limitations he's created for them.'"

After brunch, Filmmaker A wandered aimlessly for hours. There were films she had planned to see at the festival but she no longer felt like it. It was in those years that her habit of wandering, those long walks without beginning or end, began in earnest. The empty hours of thinking, questioning and reflection. Every artistic idea she had ever made use of had been thrown into her head during the space and melancholy freedom of those walks. There were so many people she could be meeting, so many connections to be made at the festival, it felt like a wasted opportunity to spend her time just wandering. But, at the same time, this feeling of intense wastefulness made the wandering all that much more delicious.

She thought about what the distributor had said, how things in a film can become reality. And how he must have meant, in some sense, that reality is society, reality is whatever we all agreed it is. This didn't relate to some core scientific idea of reality, to the fact that a chair was solid and you could sit on it, but to something more general and ever changing. She liked the idea that films could be important, could change the world, though she didn't quite believe it. She suspected the things films were allowed to bring into reality were only things already there, things that reinforced the status quo. Sharks were already threatening, and *Jaws* simply increased and solidified this general preconception. But if it was possible to bolster the status quo, then it must also be possible to undermine it. If reality was malleable, then it must be malleable in many different directions.

She walked, letting her mind wander down many such unproductive avenues. The walking and thinking felt analogous, turning this way and that, without direction but always going somewhere, turning down any street that seemed intriguing. She found herself in a shop, at first unsure what kind of shop it was, browsing shelves full of designer knick-knacks. The owner, or at least the man behind the counter she assumed was the owner, asked her if she was looking for anything in particular and she said no. But then she reconsidered. She was feeling a bit crazy from all the wandering and thought anything was worth a try.

"Do you have anything that can help me?" she asked.

"How do you mean?"

"I don't know. I just thought maybe you had something that might help."

He stared straight at her. Was she crazy? Or rather, how crazy was she? After a long moment of looking, it seemed to her that he decided she was relatively harmless.

"Let me think about it for a moment," he said.

She turned back to the shelves and continued to browse. But then another thought occurred, she had noticed the owner's skin colour, and she turned back.

"Are you by any chance Iranian? From Tehran?"

"No. Why do you ask?"

"I'm sorry. No reason. It's just I've been thinking about Tehran a lot lately."

"Have you ever been there?"

"No."

They looked at each other again for a long moment.

"Would it be impolite if I were to ask you where you are from?" she finally said.

"My family is originally from Peru, I think that's what you're asking, but I've lived in New York my entire life."

"Yes, of course." Now that she'd started, she really wanted this to go somewhere. She had the sudden, unrealistic hope that it might somehow turn into an interesting or even important encounter. "Have you ever heard of the Iranian filmmaker Abbas Kiarostami?"

"No. Who is he?"

"There's a film festival right now. And he was supposed to come for a premiere. But they turned him away at the border."

"Stuff like that happens all the time."

"Like what?"

"We turn people away."

She considered this. Did the fact that it happened all the time change anything, make it any less significant? She wanted him to explain something to her. He was a complete stranger but she felt irrationally certain that he knew something that could help. He stood looking at her in perplexed silence. The only thing she could think was to ask more questions.

"But then how do you feel about it?"

"I don't know. It's a border. You can't let in everyone."

"But Kiarostami is important. An internationally recognized auteur."

"I see. Well, it was probably just a mistake."

"You think it was a mistake?"

"I mean, not a pure mistake. The border guards in this country are obviously racist. But it's the kind of racism that happens all the time."

"Yes, that's true. I suppose it does." She wanted to continue but the conversation had clearly hit a dead end. After a moment of reflection, she turned back to the shelves, picked up an object almost at random, took it to the counter and paid for it, mainly in order to give him some business, but also to give a clear ending to their exchange. He smiled at her warmly as he handed over her change and the receipt.

Life should be more interesting, she thought to herself as she was leaving the shop. I wish there was something I could do to make life more interesting.

8. As Close as Possible to Absolute Sincerity

Write me about ordinary things that will make me feel tender and
give me hope.

—Nicole Brossard

We didn't count how many had been killed. There was no time
so instead we guessed. I guessed one hundred. She guessed
seventy-five. And they were gone so what did it matter. The
entire operation had been an utter and total catastrophe. Every
stage of the plan took a turn for the worse and the worst was
exactly what happened. There was no reason for anyone to be
dead but this lack of reason suddenly didn't matter at all. We
knew one thing: we had to escape. The outfits had been thrown
in a bin along the way, several hours ago. She poured the lighter
fluid and I set fire to an old newspaper and tossed it on top. We
would miss those outfits most of all. They were the whole fucking point of this disaster but there was no time for any of that
now. We would go back to our normal clothes. If we survived
there would be opportunity to mourn everything later, when
things blew over, if or when the world finally forgot.

And then there was the incredibly stupid part. We were in Japan, lost, deep in the countryside. We had no map. We were travelling by bicycle. The bicycles were of course stolen. We might as well have still been wearing the fucking outfits for all the good their sudden absence did us, since we were the only white people for miles and therefore painfully conspicuous in every way. I had said that bicycles were an extremely slow and laborious way to escape. She had said that it would seem more like we were tourists and that no one would be looking for a happy couple riding bicycles through the countryside. I liked that she called us a couple. I liked the idea of tourism as a disguise. I liked any idea that could take my mind off what had just happened and what we had done. I was excited by what we had done and didn't want to admit it to myself. I was appalled by my own excitement and this condition only served to make the excitement more palpable. I was pedalling calmly and smoothly, every downward pressure on the pedal an announcement to the world: Please don't pay any attention, everything is fine and calm. She was pedalling just slightly ahead of me and I watched the back of her head, feeling the warmest feelings imaginable. I wondered if tonight we would once again sleep in the same bed.

The landscape was green and lush and calm. It was a landscape that could not believe or take in what had just happened to us, or what we had done, as we bicycled through and alongside it. We had no destination but didn't want to be caught. We knew only what we didn't want, and knew that without some positive goal, a goal that we were able to formulate and then activate, the situation would remain deeply impossible.

We were not the only approach, not the only endeavour.

There were different approaches, different endeavours. And much like stubborn individuals, each approach employed strikingly different means, frameworks and strategies. Our approach was relatively straightforward: We were persecuted and would fight back.

As I biked, a few feet behind her, I once again considered the diagnosis and wondered how much longer I had to live, wondered if I should tell her, when I should tell her, how she would react. The diagnosis had given me newfound courage in our revolutionary fight. If I was going to die anyway, and sooner rather than later, why not go down in a blaze of world-changing flames. How much violence is it acceptable to utilize in service of a revolutionary cause? Were we only reacting against the violence being done to us? And if you are only reacting against something, as opposed to fighting for something, does this in some sense make the endeavour more suspect? Without the outfits, with the outfits in the trash, burned away, all these questions took on a new lucidity.

I had worn the mascot almost constantly for the past twenty years. There were very few moments when I was without it, or at least without having it close by, ready to return to my flesh like a second skin. Of course, that was not how it seemed to me at the time. I never thought of 'outfits.' As far as I was concerned, at any given moment, I was Mascot. And with the outfit gone, on this bicycle, so far away from home, suddenly I had to face the possibility that I was not. Or not only. That if I were to survive, the life ahead of me might be something else. But why did I still imagine I might survive. I was thinking only of the police, not of the disease, unsure which was a more immediate danger.

I watched her back, her legs, as she pedalled a few feet

ahead of me. She was stronger than me, not prone to such constant doubts. For her the basic premise was clear, unshakable. Even questions of strategy did not faze her. We must fight bravely and without mercy. We were vastly outnumbered but the impossible could happen and we might still prevail. I had never been so deeply in love with anyone as I was now with her and knew I would most likely never be again. There had been moments in the past, moments of weakness, when I no longer cared whether we won or lost, when all I wanted was for her not to die, not to be killed. She had many other lovers, men and women – I had no conception of the details, and at times it had bothered me, but right now, bicycling along this path, on the run, with no one we knew for miles, I couldn't have cared less. For now she was mine, whether she knew it or not.

I remembered reading: Man should not have thrown himself into this amazing adventure that is history. Everything that he does turns against him because he wasn't made to do something, he was made solely to look and to live as the animals and the trees do.

And this: I feared that the animals regarded man as a creature of their own kind which had in a highly dangerous fashion lost its healthy animal reason – as the mad animal, as the laughing animal, as the weeping animal, as the unhappy animal.

Of course we were not animals, but we related to animals most. We were man-made animals, artificial, synthetic. When we fought, we fought with the savagery of beasts who fight not to acquire or pump themselves up with worldly pride, but only for survival. We related to animals because more than anything we wanted to survive, survive on our own terms and with the nobility of natural selection. But I now had to admit to myself

168

that I, personally, would not survive. And I wondered if there was still any way to utilize my demise, to make it productive for our cause.

I watched her legs as they pedalled smoothly and easily. She had many other lovers, but so had I. I'd had my outbursts of severe jealousy over the years, but so had she. There had been periods when we were sleeping together and other periods during which we were not, but never had there been a time, from the moment I first met her, when I was not in love. Why were we in Japan? How did we end up here? I knew that I ended up here because of her.

Often the idea of survival is mentioned in relation to capitalism, as in the phrase 'economic survival' or the thought 'I need to earn money to survive.' However, in our endeavour we hoped to sever survival from economy, striving for a purer form of modernized surviving. Our fight would be a fight for survival and the fighting itself would be our life, not in the sense of employment but in the sense of a full reality with all of the inherent risk, complexity and completion that living implies. And not only in fighting, but also in the joys of love, of danger, of moving in unison, undifferentiated from one another within the pleasure of our Mascot second skins, side by side, together within the pack.

The Japanese landscape spread around us as we pedalled. We didn't see another soul and this was something of a relief since it also meant that no one had seen us. She turned down a dirt road and I followed. We had no idea where we were or where we were going, so one path was as valid as the next. I believe she chose this one because it seemed thin, obscure, leading away from civilization and into the woods. We had stolen good, sturdy bikes and, if we had to break away from roads and paths altogether, the bikes would serve us well.

There had been only a single instance, and this was many years ago, when I honestly questioned the possibility of our ongoing love, a moment when she was entranced by the man chained to the radiator. Jealousy is a terrible savagery and I tried to experience my own with as much generosity as possible. I liked the man chained to the radiator. He was fascinated by us and, in turn, we were equally fascinated by him. I wondered where he was now. We had scattered everywhere and scattered was exactly how I felt. I wondered if she also wondered where he was. I never knew to what extent she loved him. For a while it was her job to watch over him and that was what she did. Maybe that was all, but what did it matter now? They spoke together with such a deep complicity. I had never asked her if the man chained to the radiator changed anything between us, though of course at times I feared he did. Was there any pretext I could arrive at for asking her now? He was the only one of us that never wore the outfit and yet, by the end, there was no question he was one of us.

She stopped just ahead of me as I pulled up beside her. I realized it was time to eat. We laid our bikes against a tree and spread out a picnic. The picnic seemed quaint when compared to the violence of just a few hours ago. Was it really only a few hours ago? I looked at my wrist, but was no longer wearing a watch. I hadn't been paying attention, wasn't sure how long we had been biking. Maybe for most of a day. It wasn't starting to get dark, but it stayed light until quite late this time of year. As we ate I tried to calculate how much food we had stolen and how long it would last. If we were careful I thought we'd be all right for the next couple of days. We ate in silence. We often spent our time together in silence. We had said so much already, knew each other so well, often already knowing what the other would say. In battle this silent complicity had time and again served us well.

But now there was something she didn't know. Or maybe she already sensed it. I wondered if there was any point in telling her. Would it make our remaining time more precious or would it only make it sad? How would she react? I knew how she would react to almost anything, everything, but suddenly I felt unsure how she would react to this. How do animals care for their dying? We rarely had time for such dilemmas. Most often we were killed in battle: surviving our wounds or dying off fast. I feared mine would be a slower, more painful, journey.

After we finished eating we quickly made love on the blanket before getting back on our bicycles, setting off once again. I knew if I was willing she would ride all night, but also that sooner or later I would suggest we sleep. The point was to get as far away from the crime scene as possible. To ride all night would be exhausting but satisfying. I wanted this satisfaction, but was concerned that, later, if we were to find ourselves under attack, we should not be too exhausted, that we should rest now, while we could, conserve our energy for when we might need it the most. But, if I were honest with myself, that was not my main concern. More than anything I wanted to curl up beside her and sleep through the night, intertwined, as we had done so many times before, in the drowsy comfort that the future might continue to exist.

In the distance, just coming into view, we could see a building, a temple. I believe I saw it first, maybe she did, but neither of us commented on the fact. Soon we could hear the first wisp of chanting in the distance. She was a few feet ahead of me, so I found it difficult to intuit her reaction, but for me the sounds had a striking, divisive effect. On the one hand I found them calming, magical. On the other I felt a surge of fear that we would be spotted, conspicuous, that our presence calmly bicycling past the temple would allow our pursuers to close in. But as we drew closer, as the chanting increased in proximity, its steadiness washed over me and my fears decreased. For a moment I wanted to stop, join in, though I realized this was completely out of the question. Maybe the diagnosis had added a touch of mysticism to my character. They say that happens when you have evidence you will soon die. For all I knew that was the first, perhaps only, reason for the existence of religion. Moments later the voices had already peaked and were receding.

As they faded into the distance, now confident that we had passed without notice, I wondered about those inside. They were following a tradition that had been in effect for thousands of years. Ours was a much younger endeavour, but we hoped against hope it would last just as long. What might Mascots look like one thousand, two thousand, three thousand years from now? It was insanity to even wonder about such things, but as we biked there was little distraction from such vague wonderings. I wasn't part of the first generation, but all members of the first generation who had not been killed in battle, remained. You could talk to them: about their reasons, about what it had been like. How would it be when such reasons were thousands of years in the past?

I believed, desired, that there would be Mascots deep into

the future. Our idea was too strong, the courage behind it too ferocious, for us to ever completely disappear. I was part of the second generation. But already the third, fourth and fifth were finding new ways, weapons, strategies. They killed silently, quickly, planned ahead in great detail, more swiftly escaped. Watching them in battle, fighting alongside them, more and more, I realized something previously invisible: that my generation had thrived on the fierce spectacle of confrontation, our outfits splattered in blood, out in the open, outnumbered with nowhere to hide. That was when we discovered how the pack could fucking surge, when the insanity of our endeavour exploded into violence, into glory, in all directions, though no one would have said so at the time. It's only in watching the new ones, how they've learned from our mistakes, that the facts become clear. That our pleasure in open battle was also the weakness crippling us, our most intense reasons for existing drawing out, line by line, the story of our demise. So much has changed since then. This evening I am calmly bicycling across Japan. Others are in Venezuela, Portugal, Russia, Switzerland. There is no central command and no way to trace us. We are everywhere and nowhere. Outfits are abandoned, flights are booked, and later new outfits are found – an act considered unthinkable by the first generation and blasphemous for my own. But we will fight and in fighting we change and in changing we will survive.

I could still hear the faintest of chanting far behind us, peaceful as a memory, and watching her back I could feel that she held on to it as well. Twenty minutes ago were unseen monks chanting within their temple and much further back was a street full of bodies that we had injured and killed. The peacefulness of one blotted out the violence of the other. I had never before killed large numbers of civilians. I had only shot soldiers and police. This felt different, but then again not so different. The people you killed were gone, regret would not bring them back. They were gone and soon, perhaps sooner than I could imagine, I would be gone as well. But when I died someone else would wear my outfit and when he died someone else would do the same and in this way Mascots would last forever and through them, in some sense, I would persevere as well.

My legs were starting to feel tired. I tried to remember the last time I had been on a bicycle, maybe when I was a child or teenager. I remembered almost nothing of my childhood, our struggle had beaten all memories out of me. But as I stared at her back I began to remember something about her childhood, something she had once told me, shortly after we first met. I have no idea why I remembered this, but she was young, maybe seven or eight, and her father had taken her to the zoo. She wasn't sure how but believed, even then, she had already heard of the Mascots, maybe some children at school had said something. And she was staring at the animals when she said to her father, thinking the words as they came out of her mouth: "It's not right, they shouldn't be in cages like that," and her father, a kind man, a bit of a philosopher, had replied, without giving it a second thought: "One way or another we're all in cages, what we need to do is learn how to fly within them."

That moment had always stayed with her. She thought it was what she was still trying to do, find some way to live that didn't feel caged. When she told me the story I remember replying that I didn't think those were my reasons. I didn't know what my reasons were, but those didn't feel like them. And she smiled.

It was starting to get dark now, finally, and also cold. After a while we stopped to put on warmer clothes, but then immediately resumed biking. What were my reasons, my motives? When you do something for a long time, eventually, it becomes your life. Reasons become irrelevant. But the outfits were gone, we were lost, the future was uncertain in every possible aspect and all of these questions were, once again, thrashing through my mind. Maybe my reasons had mainly been to stop such questions from thrashing. When you were fighting for your life, when any moment a bullet might tear through you, there was no time to wonder. The fear was addictive, the wanting to survive, to prevail. Every small victory infused new recruits, and every Mascot added was one step away from extinction. The goals were immediate and clear. I needed that. I believed in that immediacy. It was the immediacy of being animal.

I was tired but felt the longer I held out, the more reasonable it would seem when I eventually suggested we stop for the night. It was a little game we were playing, with each other, with our survival. To go to the point of complete exhaustion might mean to save ourselves, but also to place ourselves in greater danger. I thought this might be our last stand but had felt this way so many times before. The thought passed through my mind like a mild annoyance. There was still much need for courage, since tonight, when we finally stopped to rest, I would tell her about the diagnosis. There was no point in hiding it any longer.

9. Polyamorous Love Song

The most effective lie is always the one closest to the truth. The closer the better. A dream is not true but is never a lie. There are various approaches for understanding dreams: as evidence of some deeper psychological truth, as alternate realities, as subtle yet surreal mental reprocessings of our daily lives, as experiences equally valid to those had while awake. Due to the acuity of their strangeness, dreams practically call out for interpretation. However, since we don't accurately know what consciousness is, since we don't know precisely what or how we experience being awake, why would we be able to know what happens when we dream? There are also various approaches one might use for understanding a lie. But one aspect generally agreed upon is that to tell the complete truth, and only the complete truth, at all times, is a disaster. There are different ways of being honest.

This is a dream about the day Paul decided to start writing down his thoughts. Prior to that moment he had felt there was no point. Thinking was an end in itself. There was no need for it to be recorded or glorified. But then, suddenly, he was writing books, publishing them. For a moment this shift felt like a betrayal, like he was betraying his former self, but then, at the same time, it felt positive, like a positive shift in his life. What is this concept of selling out? Is it better to hold fast to one's former ideas, or to be open to new ways of thinking about oneself and the world? If I am working as an activist to protect the environment, and a large corporation offers me a job with a generous salary to do things that will essentially harm the environment, then the situation feels rather clear. But if I believe in not making art and then, later, change my mind, the parameters of the compromise are somewhat more ambiguous. Art complicates everything.

During these years, Paul thought a lot about the question of betrayal. Though, to say the least, it had a nasty reputation, there was some sense in which betrayal was essential. To use the simplest possible analogy: If you are living in thirties Germany and all your friends are joining the Nazi party, the best thing to do would be to betray their trust in order to fight for something else. But of course nothing in real life is so simple. And here he was using Nazis again, his perennial, but least favourite, example.

He was haunted by a line he once read in an interview with Genet: "Anyone who's never experienced the pleasure of betrayal doesn't know what pleasure is." Was this the pleasure he was experiencing when he finally decided to reject his former conceptions around thinking and instead produce?

Of course the Nazi example was somehow wrong-headed, was using the word betrayal not in its usual sense. One did not 'betray' a community or society. Against an entire society it was not betrayal, it was treason. (Treason was a form of betrayal, but that was another kind of question.) No, one betrayed a

178

friend or lover. One betrayed trust. And yes, perhaps it was also possible to betray an idea.

He tried to remember: What was the exact idea he now felt he had betrayed? What were its dimensions? What precisely had it felt like? Just then the phone rang. It was Silvia. They had been living apart for the past few years, but they'd been talking about living together again. Her book had been a striking success, considerably more successful than his own. This had created tension between them and they had decided to live in separate cities for a while. It alarmed him how petty he could be. Or insecure. Back before he was making art he never remembered being so insecure. But perhaps, in itself, the decision not to make art was a form of insecurity. As they talked, Paul noticed how great Silvia sounded. He never remembered her being so convivial and relaxed when they were living together. There had always been an edge in her voice, in her stance, and now he thought that discomfort had basically come from him, or from the dynamic between them.

"But we'll see each other at the book fair in New York."

"That's true. It will be nice to spend some time together in New York again."

"Did I tell you I got asked to write an article about the Mascots?"

"I'm sorry?"

"An article. For *Atlantic Monthly*. About the Mascots. How they've changed strategy, been spotted in Portugal, Egypt, Japan."

Paul thought back to the crumpled photograph he used to carry around in his jacket pocket. He couldn't quite remember when he had first found it. Maybe when he was twenty,

twenty-one. At the time the Mascots had represented something for him, something absolutely pure. They were artists and not artists. They were absolutely loyal to something even more absolutely absurd. They risked their lives. There was a conviction even more essential than his own previous compulsion not to make art. He knew so little about them.

He didn't like the idea of Silvia writing about the Mascots, publicizing them, questioning them. For Paul, the Mascots were best back when he first heard about them, when they were barely a rumour, hardly existed. But as he continued to speak on the phone with Silvia he chose not to share these concerns. He didn't want to fight anymore, knew his criticisms cut more deeply than intended. Were they really going to live together again?

Around that time I was thinking a great deal about pop music. I had the idea that most already existing love songs, mainstream or otherwise, were directed towards one person, the ultimate soulmate or new excitement, and maybe a polyamorous love song, a love song directed towards a few (or many) soulmates, might undermine some basic songwriting assumptions. I dreamed of these not-yet-existing love songs, wondering what they would actually sound like, who might write them and who might listen.

Pop music is the gasoline of monogamy. Love songs are propaganda for monogamy. Writing is another form of loneliness. These are all statements that feel relatively true, that feel true in their gestures of empty, highly personal, provocation. Statements whose truth-value is little more than an opening for debate. Songwriting is a strange kind of writing. I remember something I once heard Darren Hayman (from the band

Hefner) say in an interview, that people often complimented him on his lyrics, and he was flattered by this, but he had always been more interested in writing tunes. Because a song could have bad lyrics and a great melody and still be a good song. But if a song had great lyrics and a terrible melody, the entire endeavour was kind of doomed. How would we experience love if pop culture did not exist?

There is no need to explain how I escaped from the Mascots. I had no desire to escape. They abandoned me. If I'd had my way I would have spent the rest of my life chained to that radiator. No need to explain how or why I wrote a book about my time with them, how the book brought them much unwanted notoriety and, of course, worsened their general predicament, placing them in much greater danger. That, I suppose, was my great betrayal. Yet it also brought me the success I had always craved. I had read each of Paul's books, astonished that I'd previously been so mistaken about him, that he had not dedicated his life to the brilliant privacy of his own thoughts, but instead decided to share them. We were both very young back then, it was too soon to tell where we would eventually land. Paul now writes and publishes, so he can no longer look down at me for publishing, but I am certain he would never approve of me writing a popular book about my time in captivity. The Mascots wouldn't approve either. I don't care, I'm no longer looking for approval. I stand behind what I've done. For me, in the years following my abandonment, in the years after they no longer wished to have me around, it was a necessity.

From time to time I wonder where they are. The ones I knew and the ones I didn't. The ones who are still alive. I miss them. I want them to survive, to persevere, but it is hard for me to imagine. It is hard to imagine how their revolution will ever succeed, how, after all the chaos and violence they have brought into the world, they will ever be able to live in peace, as they sometimes claimed to wish, that their outfits will ever be accepted as a natural, ordinary part of the modern world. But successful or not, whatever becomes of them, they had ripped through our lives and none of us would ever be the same. That is how I ended my book: They had ripped through our lives and none of us would ever be the same. It didn't bother me that it was a sentimental ending. I believe there are times for genuine sentiment, in journalism as in life.

Love songs attempt to describe how we feel when we're in love. But as they're describing, they are also telling us how we should feel, creating norms we can compare to our own experiences, giving us language that helps us describe a realm of emotion that in some sense is always beyond language. Many of these songs are written in about five minutes and yet we can listen to them over and over again for years. Love songs are about desire, but they are also, often, about loyalty. In some ways romantic love is the passage from desire towards loyalty. But maybe the polyamorous love songs that I dream might some day exist will complicate such dualities, generating nuances closer to our daily reality in which, if we are open to life, conflicting thoughts, questions and desires continuously surprise us.

Paul and Silvia did see each other again in New York and neither could remember when they'd last had such a wonderful time together. And it was during that visit they did something they had never done before. One night, lying in bed, they started describing, telling stories about, all the other people they had slept with during the time they were together. Neither of them could believe just how enjoyable these stories were, mainly because they had happened so long ago and whatever jealousy had existed was now ancient history.

But jealousy is perhaps the wrong word. They were jealous of each other's books, but less so with other lovers. And this might have been what connected them most, and would keep them close until the end. In the past, they'd both had to overcome something in order to begin writing: Paul, his own belief in thinking as an end in itself; Silvia, her relationship with new filmmaking and its mentor. Before they could begin telling stories they'd had to break free. And now they had all these juicy stories to tell each other, stories that concerned them both, that were tied up in the fact that they 'weren't really a couple' and that they were now telling each other for the first time.

Have you ever had a dream in which nothing unusual happens? A dream in which you simply do ordinary things in an ordinary way and there is nothing particularly 'dream-like' about it? Such dreams are fascinating in their apparent lack of imagination. What might they be trying to tell us? That ordinary reality is enough and does not require wild elaborations? That the richest symbolism is to be found within the most banal details? That we are boring? I am thinking of dreams in which one is simply driving a car and then wakes up. Or a dream in which one pleasantly enacts all the routine tasks of a normal day at the office. It seems that in such dreams it is not the car or the job that carry the symbolic value, but instead the very normality of the dream itself. These dreams hold up a mirror to reality, and ask us if there is any meaning or strangeness added to an object simply because it takes place within a reflection.

It would be impossible to gather statistics around such questions, but I wonder what percentage of all the dreams that occur in the world might fall into this 'normal' category. When we are awake, on rare occasions, something incredibly dream-like might happen to us, and when we are asleep, perhaps with equal rarity, we can have an analogously un-dreamlike experience. So I find myself wondering: What if the proportions were reversed, much as they have been for the past hundred and eighty-three pages.

There was one particular story Silvia told that night which struck them both far more than any of the others. She had just dropped Paul off at the airport and decided to stop for a drink on the way home. The bar was half-empty and she sat at the counter nursing a gin and tonic, wondering about her life. A young woman sat down on the stool beside her. Silvia realized she had ended up at the queer bar, one of the places she used to frequent years ago. She had come here out of habit, without realizing it, almost as if she had slipped back in time. They started to talk. The young woman was flirting and Silvia was smiling and drinking and starting to enjoy herself. She realized this woman had read her book, it had just come out, and was also something of a fan. Silvia couldn't remember a time when someone had chatted her up because she was famous, perhaps this was the first time ever, and this sense of newness, also a slight feeling of power, drove a surge of excitement straight through their flirtation. And then, out of the blue, without knowing why, Silvia said: "Would you like to kiss me? Right now? Here?" The young woman beside her seemed hesitant, so Silvia let it drop, didn't press the matter. But they had another drink and another, continued to talk about random, unimportant things, smiling and making eye contact, and a few minutes later, spontaneously, without warning, the young woman leaned over and kissed Silvia, one long wonderful kiss, then slipped away from the bar stool and bolted out of the room, ran off, straight out of the bar.

There was a song playing over the sound system that Silvia loved. She didn't remember which song exactly. But she remembered that it was playing and it was a song she loved. And thinking back, Silvia felt that perhaps that kiss was one of the kisses she would remember most in her entire life. Because it was only a single, perfect moment in time. Because it didn't lead to anything more. And if she ever heard the song again she would instantly remember that moment. She told Paul this story and Paul listened as they lay in bed together and they both felt that this was one of the stories they would come back to, that it would be one of the many anecdotes, many shortcuts, that were like a kind of secret code between them, but they didn't yet know for what.

Acknowledgements

It would have been impossible for me to complete this book without the generous support of three international writing residencies. I would very much like to thank the Danish Centre for Writers and Translators at Hald Hovedgaard in Viborg, the International House of Literature Passa Porta in Brussels, and Alkàntara in Lisbon, as well as those who invited me and made my stays so hospitable and productive, including: Peter Q. Rannes, Ilke Froyen, Thomas Walgrave and Ana Riscado. Plus all the amazing writers and artists I met along the way.

Sections from this book have been previously published in *Le Livre de chevet*, *Fence*, *Gone Lawn* and *Lemon Hound*.

Godfrey Cheshire quotations from the December 29th, 1999, issue of *New York Press*. Jean Genet quotation from *Prisoner of Love*. Unattributed quotations on page 168 from an interview with E.M. Cioran in *Writing at Risk: Interviews in Paris with Uncommon Writers* by Jason Weiss and, I believe, from Friedrich Nietzsche, though I am no longer able to find or verify the source. Very special thanks to Terry Tempest Williams for permission to print her letter in full.

The author wishes to thank the Canada Council for the Arts for their support in the form of a travel grant.

Colophon

Distributed in Canada by the Literary Press Group www.lpg.ca.
Distributed in the United States by Small Press Distribution
www.spdbooks.org.
Shop online at www.bookthug.ca.

BOOK
PRODUCTION
WAR ECONOMY
STANDARD

Cover painting by Matthew Palladino.
Type and design by Malcolm Sutton.